A SHOT AT LOVE

MILLER FAMILY MEDICAL
BOOK 1

DAPHNE JAMES HUFF

A Shot at Love

DAPHNE JAMES HUFF

For my wonderfully supportive husband, who followed me to Boston for a job.

ONE

ANAIS

There were many things Dr. Anais Miller loved about the Floodline Brewery. It was walking distance from her house. They had the yummiest fruited sours within fifty miles. Their homemade ice cream was the best in a hundred. "A pint with your pint" was their sales pitch, and it made her chuckle every time she walked in.

It wasn't the ice cream or the beer that made it her favorite place in town, however. It was because it felt like home. None of the bars she'd frequented in Seattle during medical school and residency could even come close. It wasn't because of the décor —which, frankly, was a little too clean and minimalist after the most recent renovation. It was because the Hayes family, who owned it, were all family friends, so there was always someone there to talk to. Isabelle and Carter Hayes had gone to school with Anais and her twin brother Bastien, and they were two of her best friends in the world.

Frowning, she looked around, but couldn't spot either of them behind the bar.

Which was odd, since the place was packed with every single other person in the small town of Jasper Creek, Colorado.

The tables were full. People were standing behind the bar three deep, and the energy of the crowded room was high. It had to be something good.

It *was* the first day of fall break, but the crowd was more than just the teachers letting off some steam.

"Whoa, what's going on?" Anais asked the person closest to her. "The World Series doesn't start for another week, right?"

With two brothers who loved sports, she followed them whether she wanted to or not.

"The freezer in the kitchen broke so Mrs. Hayes is giving away ice cream for free."

A smile spread across Anais's face. Her day hadn't been the best, and she'd come in looking for the comfort of the Floodline and a chat with Isabelle.

Free ice cream would be an acceptable substitute.

Getting to the bar to order took some time, since she had to stop and say hello to nearly everyone.

"Anais, I have this lump, could you take a quick check?"

"Dr. Miller, great, I wanted to ask, Preston is teething and she has a fever . . ."

"Oh, good thing I ran into you. I'll be late to my appointment Thursday. Should I call the office, or can you tell Clementine?"

The line between professional and personal in Jasper Creek was extremely blurry. Since getting back into town a few months ago, Anais had been working on firming it up without making much progress. Still, she wasn't quite ready to give up her efforts. She gave everyone a patient smile, and answered their questions the way a Dr. Miller should—the way her dad, Dr. James Miller III, would expect her to do.

Her stomach clenched tight at the thought of her dad. Their fight earlier today was still top of mind. What she thought was good news had sent him into a tizzy she hadn't expected. They'd always been so close, it felt like the sun was rising in the west to be at odds with him. If she didn't get some ice cream soon, she might start crying in the middle of the brewery.

Finally, she eased her way past the biggest group of people blocking the bar and grabbed the last open stool. Shoulder to shoulder with the people next to her, she flashed a friendly smile to the familiar face on her left.

When she turned to her right, Anais was shocked to see someone she didn't recognize. She couldn't claim to know all three thousand residents of her town personally, but she knew all the adults by sight—and everyone her age by name. The men had all been categorized and analyzed as potential partners, and she'd done the same for Isabelle with all the women.

She knew with absolute certainty that she'd never met this mystery man before.

The first thing she noticed were the impressively wide deltoids that his gray t-shirt strained against. Looking up, she took in his sharp jawline covered in blond stubble, then the downward tilt of his full lips. It was too dark in the bar to see the color of his eyes, but it was easy to see the strain in them, the two deep lines in between his eyebrows giving a menacing air to his features.

When his eyes met hers, Anais put on her best "welcome to our town" smile. The two lines deepened.

"No ice cream for you?" Anais asked, gesturing to his lonely looking pint of beer.

He blinked once, and Anais's pulse quickened as his gaze shifted to take in her features.

"Pardon?"

Ignoring the flickering excitement making its way through her veins, Anais gestured around the room. "Everyone here is taking advantage of the free ice cream. Isn't that why you're here?"

"I'm waiting for a friend." The man checked his watch, then folded his thick arms across his formidable pectorals. "He's late."

"Probably just looking for parking." Anais shook her head. "I've never seen it this packed before. I bet some ice cream would help pass the time."

He raised an eyebrow.

"And your mood." She grinned.

At that, his lips ticked up. "I'm sorry, I didn't mean to be rude. I just drove in from Denver, and I'm exhausted."

Her heart squeezed in sympathy. Denver was close enough for day trips, but far enough away that most people in Jasper Creek couldn't work there. Her mom made the trip every day for her job as head of radiology at a major university hospital there, but Dr. Heather Miller had always done things a little differently than everyone else. Anais was much happier trodding the more familiar paths in life, like her dad.

"The traffic must have been terrible the day before fall break. No wonder you're tired." She gave him a sly smile. "The sugar in ice cream can help with that."

He chuckled, the sound warm and thick as honey. Anais held back a shiver.

"You seem pretty set on getting me some ice cream." There was the slightest hint of an accent in his voice, in the long and luxurious way he lingered on the "i" in ice cream. "Anything you'd recommend?"

Anais shifted into consultation mode, thrilled to be asked for food rather than medical advice. "First of all, any issues with lactose? Any allergies I should be aware of?" She didn't want to send this gorgeous man to the hospital due to her lack of attention.

He shook his head, eyes glinting, a smile playing on his lips.

"What's your favorite movie?"

"What does that have to do with ice cream?" he asked, tilting his head.

"Everything!" She threw up her hands. "If you're a romcom guy, then I'd suggest cookies and cream, obviously."

"Obviously."

"If you like superhero movies, then there's the blueberry and cherry vanilla swirl."

"Because it's red, white, and blue?"

"Naturally."

The smile spreading across his face was distractingly handsome, but Anais had spent too much time working on her ice cream and movie matching to waste this chance to use it on someone who'd never heard it before.

"Foreign films are sea salt caramel." She held up her fingers and ticked them off so she wouldn't forget one. "Comedies are butterscotch, musicals are cotton candy, and historical dramas are hazelnut."

"What about sports movies?"

Her brother Bastien was a former athlete, and she'd purposely left that category out just to annoy him. She considered the man for a moment, taking in his muscled form and sweatpants, analyzing the possibilities and arriving at the only logical conclusion.

"You mean like *Rocky*?"

"Or *A League of Their Own*."

The floor seemed to fall away from her as her stomach dropped. "Is that really your favorite movie?"

"It's in the top five." His lips had taken on a mischievous curl and Anais's stomach fluttered. It had been so long since she'd been flirted with by anyone in town. She was either Dr. Miller, someone who could look at a weird spot on your back, or she was Bastien's sister. She was never someone to banter with at the bar.

"Is that your way of admitting your number one is *Rocky*?"

"Do I still get your ice-cream recommendation if I say yes?"

Anais laughed. "That's too easy. Rocky Road."

"Could I get you a scoop?"

The accent had become more noticeable, a slow drawl full of dropped Rs. His voice was smooth and lilting, like a slow swim through warm, moonlit waters. It reminded Anais of her college roommate, freshman year. She'd been a political science major from South Carolina who'd liked *You've Got Mail* and butter pecan.

"Sure." The smile on Anais's face was probably ridiculous, but her night had just gotten way better, no ice cream needed.

He waved at Matt, one of the two Hayes cousins who were working behind the bar. They both looked like they needed a few pints themselves to get over the mad rush. When the mystery man held out a twenty in a hand the size of her face, Matt waved it away, explaining everything was free. As soon as Matt turned to put the order into the tablet computer next to the bar, Mr. Muscles shoved the money into the mostly empty tip jar without hesitating.

A warm swell filled Anais's chest.

He turned back to her, the teasing look still on his face. "I take it you're not a fan of *Rocky*?"

"Road? Of course I am. I love all ice cream equally."

He raised an eyebrow. "All ice cream? You rank vanilla at the same level as something with peanut butter and chocolate, like, uh . . . " He looked lost for a moment.

"Moose Tracks."

"That's an ice-cream flavor?"

"The best."

"Ha." He pointed an accusatory finger at her. They were squeezed together so tightly he nearly hit her shoulder. "You do have a favorite."

Fighting the urge to stick out her tongue, she shifted on her stool so she was just the tiniest bit closer to him. Engineering an accidental brush of his hand on her shoulder wasn't too desperate, was it? She'd have to ask Isabelle later, when she finally found her. A handsome stranger from Denver was surely worth at least a bit of embarrassing behavior.

"Why is *Rocky* your favorite?"

His eyes darted to the side. "Oh, you know, overcoming the obstacles, all that. Motivational."

She folded her arms across her chest. "I have four younger siblings, you'll have to do better than that if you want to get a lie past me."

He laughed, the sound rippling across her skin like a warm breeze.

"That was kind of a personal question, though," she said. Her hand went to her forehead to brush aside her hair. "Side effects of a big family and my job. You don't have to answer it."

The possibilities ran through her mind as she took what she already knew about him—very little—and attempted an unadvisable and unprofessional diagnosis based on it. This was the effect of an attractive man actually talking to her about something other than his prescription refill.

He flashed her a grateful smile. "Five kids must eat a lot of ice cream. What movie pairs with Moose Tracks?"

"*Legally Blonde.*"

"That's your favorite movie?" His eyes raked over her dark waves.

"It's not just blondes who have to work hard to prove they can do more than what people expect of them." It was hard to tell the color of his short hair, but based on his light stubble and matching eyebrows, he wasn't a brunet.

The half-smile he gave her was her favorite expression so

far. It was more serious than teasing, like he was looking at something rare and precious.

"Showing you're more than what people expect of you . . . it's why I love *A League of Their Own.*" He rubbed a hand on the back of his neck. "Even if I get teased something awful for it by guys nowhere near as pretty as you."

She inhaled sharply. Her eldest-sister lie detector was silent. A beat passed, and his eyes dropped to her mouth. She licked her lips, suddenly aware just how very hot the bar was when it was packed with people.

In every other area of her life, Anais always knew what to do. Her systems and plans and categorization put the world into an order she could anticipate and control.

For the first time in a long time, she wasn't sure what to do next.

Luckily, he was the one to finally break the silence.

"I'm Jackson, by the way." He held out his hand, but they were already squeezed so close together at the bar, his hand grazed her waist.

Heat flooded her face as Jackson's eyes went wide.

"Pardon me, I didn't mean to—"

"Nissy!"

Anais turned to see Isabelle coming out of the kitchen with two cups of Rocky Road in her hands. "Matt said you were out here. I need a break, I've been scooping for hours."

The urge to stay, eat ice cream, and continue chatting with Jackson was strong, but one look at Isabelle's face told Anais she had to go. Her friend looked like she was about to melt. While a few minutes of flirting had buoyed her spirits, Anais knew the fight with her dad would continue to gnaw at her like an ulcer if she didn't talk it out.

Besides, Jackson was meeting a friend and he was from Denver. There was a chance this wasn't the only time she'd see him. It was a small town, after all. Better to leave him wanting more than to let him see just how excited she was to have been properly flirted with for the first time in ages.

"I've got to go. It was nice to meet you, Jackson." She took the two cups from Isabelle and handed him one. "Thank you for the ice cream. Enjoy your evening."

Disappointment flashed across his face, before he gave her a wide smile that highlighted all his best features. It was the practiced smile of a man who knew the effect he had on women.

"Nice to meet you as well. Thank you for the ice cream and movie lesson." His eyes raked her body once quickly, then again, slower before he held her gaze while she tried not to squirm in her seat. "Maybe I'll see you around town?"

"Maybe." With a giggle and a wink, she slid off her stool and followed Isabelle to the kitchen and out the back door. She allowed herself one look over her shoulder, and she grinned when she spotted Jackson with his eyes closed and the spoon in his mouth, a look of pure pleasure on his face. She may not always know what to do around men, but she did know her ice cream.

When they were outside in the back parking lot, Isabelle looped her arm in hers. "Please tell me you didn't talk that gorgeous man's ears off about your ice-cream theories."

Anais laughed, then caught sight of her brother jogging between the cars. She waved at him to avoid answering Isabelle.

"Is all the ice cream gone?" He stopped running and leaned over, hands on his knees, panting to catch his breath. "I had to park all the way down the road by your house."

"Almost, but I saved some blueberry and cherry swirl for you." Isabelle reached down and tousled his hair.

He batted her hands away and stood up. "Sweet. Perfect way to start fall break before my hiking trip."

"You should take it easy if you'll be hiking tomorrow." Anais gave her best big-sister stare—even if she was only thirteen minutes older than her twin. "Nothing too wild."

"You sound like Dad." He rolled his eyes. "When have I ever gotten too wild at the Floodline?"

Isabelle and Anais exchanged glances and sighed in unison as he hurried off toward the bar. Once he was inside, they continued walking through the parking lot, then turned toward Anais's house down the road.

Though their conversation focused on Anais's fight with her dad, just like she needed, a part of her wished she were still back in the bar talking to Jackson.

Hopefully she'd see him again soon.

TWO
ANAIS

The pounding on the door could be the wind, Anais thought sleepily as she turned over in her bed.

Except it sounded a lot like Bastien.

With a sigh that echoed through her small house even louder than the storm outside, she dragged herself from under the covers and made her way to the front door.

"This had better be an emergency." He probably couldn't hear her from three rooms away with the weather howling, but she was sure her twin knew she was saying it.

If this was just another one of Bastien's midnight requests for pancakes on his way home from the Floodline, her brother would be getting an earful instead. She'd been having one of her favorite dreams about solving crimes with Henry Cavill, who praised her analytical mind before inviting her up to his apartment to play violin for her.

Luckily for Bastien—or rather, unluckily—when she opened the door, it was clear that this was, in fact, an emergency.

He also wasn't alone.

Of course, the first words out of her mouth, likely due to

sleep deprivation and binging too many of Mr. Cavill's movies last weekend, would be highly inappropriate.

"Those are some impressive deltoids."

The lips of the well-muscled man keeping her brother upright twitched.

Rubbing the last of the sleep out of her eyes, she realized she recognized those muscles. Seeing a slight widening of his eyes, she understood that Jackson was just as surprised to be at her door as she was to see him there.

The floor seemed to shift under her feet. She gripped the door frame for support, then looked between him and her brother. "What happened?"

All she got from Bastien was a groan that turned into a whimper.

"He fell." Jackson's eyes roamed the interior of the house, never settling on anything, and only briefly pausing on Anais when he asked, "Where should I put him?"

"Oh. Right this way." Relieved to have something to focus on other than Jackson, she ushered them in, wincing at the puddles of water they brought inside. They were both drenched, as if they'd walked miles in the rain pouring down in buckets outside, instead of the half-mile down the road from the bar.

The floor can handle a little water, she reminded herself with a calming breath. *Focus on the patient.*

"Where did he fall?"

"I slipped outside the bar," Bastien said, after taking a large, gasping breath. "On the stairs."

"You know Carter hasn't fixed those. The sheriff told him twice just this week."

Another deep, calming breath to avoid more yelling. This was why doctors shouldn't treat their own family. The temptation to nag was too strong to ignore.

A sharp cry burst from Bastien when his foot bumped against the wall.

"Sorry," said Jackson.

With a quick glance, Anais made an assessment of Jackson's state of inebriation. His eyes were clear, no sign of glassiness, and though he'd only said a few words, his deep voice wasn't slurred or hesitant. The southern accent she'd heard earlier in the bar was even stronger, the long vowels sounding almost British to her tired ears. But no, it was much more likely he was southern than a blond twin to Henry Cavill.

Also likely was that he'd bumped Bastien's leg because he was unfamiliar with the house and its narrow hallway, not because he was drunk.

While half of her was twisted in knots, completely thrown by Jackson's unexpected appearance, the other half was totally focused on her brother. His moans of pain were almost constant. Rubbing her forehead, Anais let the practical, doctor side of her take over, and she led the two men to her spare bedroom, where she instructed Jackson to place Bastien on the bed. The soft cotton bedspread was soaked and muddy in an instant.

Another deep breath.

Sheets can be washed.

It was the work of only a few seconds to roll up Bastien's soggy pant leg and remove his shoe to examine the ankle. He didn't need to tell her which one. The swelling at the site of his old injury from college was so visible, Anais felt her own ankle twinge with sympathy.

"Walk me through what happened."

Instead of answering, the two men exchanged glances for a long moment. Finally, Jackson held up his hands.

"This is all you, Bash."

Anais looked up, her heart pounding. Only Bastien's close friends and family called him that. Who was this man? She examined him again, carefully, and he shifted slightly under her intense gaze.

No, she'd definitely never seen him before tonight. Which was why she'd been so thrilled at the bar. Embarrassment trickled in at the edges of her chest to think she'd been pointlessly flirting with one of Bastien's friends, but she pushed it away.

Turning her scrutiny back to her brother, she gave a threatening weight to every letter of his name. "Bastien?"

What little color in his face drained out of it. "I wanted to race Jackson," he said in a small voice.

Narrowing her eyes she frowned at Jackson standing sentry at the door, thick arms crossed over his formidable pectorals.

"I refused," said Jackson.

Anais relaxed a little.

"Because you knew you'd lose." Bastien's voice was stronger.

"Because I didn't want to get hurt." Jackson's lips twisted, like he was trying not to smile. "Clearly, I won this race."

"You forfeited." Her brother's grating voice boomed in the small room. "I got to the bottom first. I won."

"Sliding down five steps on your ass isn't winning."

"Bet you've never slid that far to make a run."

"Wanna bet? You were at that game I played against Scranton."

"Sure, why not? You already lost once to me tonight."

Anais relaxed even more. If Bastien was up for fighting with his friend, then it couldn't be too serious of an injury.

Jackson opened his mouth to keep the battle going, but Anais cut him off to ask her brother, "Do I also need to check your glutes and back for abrasions?"

Bastien's face, which had been a worrying pale despite his heated words with Jackson, turned bright red. "No, that won't be necessary."

Which probably meant he was torn up and tender there and didn't want his sister to see it. She rolled her eyes. With practiced precision, she finished the examination of his ankle.

"It's not broken." She stood up and went to the nearby dresser to get the supplies to splint and wrap it. "It's a grade one sprain, borderline grade two."

"Why are you wrapping it if it's just a grade one?"

The question came from Jackson. When she quirked her brow at Bastien, he gave a nod to let her know she could speak freely in front of his friend. "Because of his history of ankle injuries."

"I'll still be able to go hiking though, right?" Her brother's green eyes, so similar to her own, were wide and pleading. "I've been looking forward to this for months."

"Bastien. Your parents and sister are all doctors. You played soccer throughout high school and most of college. There is no reason you shouldn't be keenly aware of your own physical limitations." After her little speech, she put a hand on her hip and raised her eyebrow at him.

All she got in response was a pout.

Sighing, she bent to start wrapping his ankle, unable to resist more lecturing, which was her right and responsibility as the oldest Miller sibling.

"You can't just assume someone will always be there to fix you up."

The problem with Bastien was that the possibility of getting hurt never entered his brain. He never considered that if his body couldn't magically heal at eighteen, it was even less likely to do so at twenty-eight.

They might be twins, but there was no question who was the more responsible one.

"Well, I'm fixed now, right? I can still go on the trip?"

"No." Anais finished wrapping his ankle and stood up,

rolling up the remaining bandage. "If it was that important, then you should have been more careful coming out of the Floodline."

Bastien's face went even redder. From his position by the door, she heard Jackson chuckle.

"Are you just going to stand there and laugh?" Bastien asked his friend.

"It doesn't look like Dr. Miller needs my help."

A sad sigh escaped her as a wave of disappointment rolled through her tired body. Despite their meeting earlier, of course her brother's gorgeous friend would only see her as a doctor. It was the sad story of her very single life.

Having handled the most urgent part of Bastien's injury, she held out her hand to him to introduce herself properly to Jackson. "You can call me Anais."

The lateness of the hour made her voice do a funny quavering thing.

His lips twitched again and she inhaled sharply. Would he tell Bastien they'd already met? Jackson inhaled deeply before he reached out his own and to shake hers. "Jackson Hart."

The R dropped on his last name, along with her stomach. Such a simple thing as his words shouldn't have such a strong effect on her.

Realization dawned on her. "Oh this is the Hart you kept talking about last week." She looked between the two men. "The baseball player you know from college who's here to hike with you."

He won't be staying now that Bastien's injured.

With a flutter in her stomach at the silly thought, Anais returned the unused bandage to the dresser next to the bed. So what if they'd hit it off at the bar? It wasn't like anything could happen. He was only there for a week. He was her brother's friend. And athletes definitely weren't her type.

Then she turned and his blue eyes met hers. The breath caught in her lungs. He had sectoral heterochromia in one eye, turning half of the blue iris brown, just like her favorite British actor.

Well, he's kind of my type.

Oblivious to his sister gawking at his friend, Bastien pouted from the bed. "He won't be hiking with me now. Unless I go really slow?" He shot a hopeful glance her way.

"Absolutely not."

"You should listen to your doctor." Jackson's deep voice wasn't loud, but he spoke like he was used to being heeded. "And your sister."

Doctuh. Sistuh.

A flutter beat its way out of her stomach into her chest. *Deep breath, concentrate on the patient.*

"I'm sure you and Jackson will figure out something else to do for the next week that doesn't involve you walking around."

Bastien threw up his hands, the bedsprings creaking beneath him. "That's literally all there is to do here."

He had a point. Jasper Creek, Colorado, wasn't close enough to one of the resorts to be popular with tourists, but the mountains were nearby, and the locals all enjoyed hiking and biking during the warmer months. Then there was fishing in Jasper Creek itself, which was too shallow and rocky for any kind of real boating activities.

Anais and Bastien's great-great-grandfather and his brother had started the Miller family's medical practice back when Jasper Creek had been the site of one of the more popular sanatoriums for tuberculosis. Thanks to antibiotics, the sanatorium had closed down. But the Millers had stayed and carried on the tradition of being doctors for the town.

Except for Bastien.

With great effort, she avoided rolling her eyes as she

wondered what their great-great-grandfather would say about the eldest son of this generation whining about not being able to hike.

"You should stay here tonight, so I can be sure you won't move it too much." She tugged at the long sleeves of her pajamas—which she only just realized were the joke set her brother had gotten her that featured pictures of ice-cream cones. Heat flooded her face. At the bar he'd called her pretty, but she was a total disaster now. No chance of any good impression remaining. "Let me get you some new clothes. And new sheets."

Keeping her eyes trained on the ground, she walked out of the room before she strangled her brother—or made an even bigger fool of herself in front of Jackson.

THREE
JACKSON

"I'm sorry you came all the way out here for nothing."

Jackson was changing the sheets on the bed so he couldn't see Bastien's face, but the distress in his friend's voice was evident. The smell of lavender invaded Jackson's nose, and he closed his eyes to inhale deeply.

He pictured Anais's eyes, bright green and focused on helping her brother.

A doctor. Why'd she have to be a doctor?

Shaking his head, he opened his eyes again. "Don't worry about it. We'll find something to do."

"You mean you'll stay?"

"Of course." Jackson turned and helped Bastien slide back into bed. Then he set the crutches provided by his sister—*why'd she have to be Bash's sister?*—right next to him on the floor within reach. "I came here to hang out with you before my surgery next week. We can do that piddling at home watching TV just as easily as hiking in the mountains."

"You didn't come here just to watch TV in the most beautiful state in the country."

Jackson chuckled at that and sat in the chair in the corner

he'd just helped Bastien out of. For as long as they'd known each other, the guy had been talking about how gorgeous Colorado was. Finally, Jackson was seeing it for himself.

All the stunning scenery he'd seen since his plane had landed last week, however, paled in comparison to Bastien's sister. Not that he'd seen much of the outdoors yet. He'd spent the whole trip so far in doctors' offices and a cheap hotel room. Hiking with Bash in Jasper Creek before his surgery was supposed to be a way to relax. He'd never expected to meet someone while waiting for his friend at the Floodline.

Anais had been pretty in the bar, but seeing her all sleepy eyed and worried about her brother took it to another level. Between those bright green eyes and dark hair—piled up on her head rather than long and loose like it had been earlier—she put the southern belles he'd grown up with to shame. All that talk of ice cream and movies had been too cute for words, but those pajamas ratcheted up her adorable factor to about a thousand.

He'd wanted to ask his friend about the girl he'd met when Bastien finally showed up at the bar, but the conversation had gone straight to sports and plans for the week. He wished he'd been a little more insistent on getting details about her—like if she was Bash's sister—before they'd unexpectedly showed up at her house.

He ran a hand over the back of his neck. "Your sister didn't seem that surprised to see you."

"Ah, she's used to me showing up after a few rounds at the Floodline." Bastien moved around in the bed and let out a hiss when he must have moved his ankle in a painful way. "She's also used to patching me up. Even in high school, she'd be next to Dad, watching him work his magic on whatever bump or scrape I'd managed to get either from soccer or just being a dumb kid in a small town without a lot to keep me busy."

The fact she was a doctor should have been enough on its

own to cool his attraction, but her no-nonsense yet tender way of dealing with Bash's ankle had intrigued him. He wondered if he'd be less anxious over his surgery if it were someone like her doing it. His team was paying for Jackson's operation at a top-ranked hospital for orthopedic surgery, so he hadn't been the one to pick the cold and brittle robot in a lab coat he'd met with in Denver the day before.

"I'm sure TV is just as good as hiking."

Bastien gave him a sour look. "The hiking is amazing. I'm so bummed we can't go."

The surgery had been unexpected, but a perfect excuse to finally visit Bastien. Once it was done, he'd be back on a plane to Arizona to rehab and watch the final games of the fall league from the sidelines.

Even if she'd been someone other than Bash's doctor sister, all Anais could have been was a vacation fling. Until Jackson was finally playing in the majors, he couldn't get distracted by anything or anyone. The invitation to the fall league had been a sign his team was finally taking a serious look at him.

"Floodline was fun. We can do that instead." He leaned forward and grinned. "Just don't hurt yourself next time."

Bastien groaned and covered his head with a pillow.

"Must be nice."

"To have doctors in the family?" His voice was muffled.

That was definitely not what Jackson had been thinking.

"To have her live so close to the bar." Though Jackson had only arrived that afternoon, he could tell the town wasn't that big. It was basically one long, winding road with a few side streets, and a small section his rideshare driver had referred to as "town center" lined with shops. It had taken less than five minutes to get from the town limit to the Floodline earlier that night, and while the walk in the rain had been miserable, it hadn't taken long to get from there to Bastien's sister's house.

Anais. Bastien had mentioned a few sisters over the years, but Jackson never really paid attention to their names. She'd pronounced it "Anna-eece" and it seemed to fit her perfectly. It was beautiful and intriguing.

"She doesn't mind you coming over? Doesn't bother her boyfriend?"

"She doesn't have one." Bastien paused in his shifting on the bed. "Why?"

"No reason."

Bastien raised an eyebrow. "I might have been in half-drunk agony before, but I noticed the way she was looking at you. Don't flirt with my sister, please. It's too weird."

Too late.

Jackson kept his face blank at the reminder that Anais was his friend's sister. There weren't many people Jackson called true friends, but his old college housemate was one of them, and he would never do anything to hurt him.

"A doctor? Please." Jackson ran a hand along the back of his neck. "Not even interested."

Bastien nodded. Jackson hadn't told him much about his family, but his friend knew enough to understand that the last person Jackson would ever pursue was someone with a medical degree. After being cut off by his surgeon parents for abandoning the Hart family traditions for the life of an athlete, he wasn't looking to dive back into the world of doctors again.

Even for someone who made his heart pound the way it did before he stepped up to the plate.

The bed creaked when Bastien shifted again. "Would you be up for fishing instead of hiking this week? Would it hurt your hand?"

Just as Jackson opened his mouth to reply, Anais appeared in the doorway and he forgot what he was about to say.

"These are some of Bastien's old clothes." Anais glanced at him coolly before looking over his shoulder at her brother.

His stomach dropped. Had she heard his comment about doctors?

Whatever spark of eagerness he'd seen in her eyes when she'd opened the door must have been due to the late night and the beers he'd had at the bar—though he was far from drunk. He never had more than a few drinks, even in the off-season when he didn't have to worry as much about the impact it could have on the game.

Still, it took longer to recover after a late night. Twenty-nine wasn't old by any means, but in the world of professional sports, it meant his body had been pushed to its limit for well over a decade. The fracture in his hand was a harsh reminder of it. If he still wanted a shot at a major league contract, then he had to be in top condition.

That was the only reason he was going through with the surgery. Until now, he'd managed to avoid all hospitals and limited his interaction with doctors to his required exams for the league. Physical therapists were the only kind of medical professional that Jackson could stand, but there was no amount of physio that could fix his fractured hamate bone. This surgery would get him back in the game within weeks rather than the months it would take without an operation.

He took the clothes from Anais and held them up.

"The shirt might be a little tight," he said to tease Bastien, who glowered at him from where he lay on the bed, but then he saw Anais's cheeks turn pink.

Maybe that spark hadn't been his imagination.

She turned to leave. "I'll go get some sheets and blankets for the couch."

Trying to put her out of his mind and focus on his friend in pain, Jackson raised an eyebrow at Bastien. "You need help changing?"

"Get out of here, Hart. I can still kick with the other leg."

Laughing, he headed into the hallway and closed the door behind him. The house wasn't big, and they'd passed the living room on the way to the spare bedroom, so he knew where to go.

It was a small space, with a couch that took up most of the room and a tiny coffee table. There was no door, just an open archway to the hallway. He couldn't change there, but he didn't want to just start opening doors to find the bathroom. He turned to go find Anais, and bumped smack dab into her.

"Sorry." He grabbed hold of her shoulders to keep her from toppling over. Their eyes locked, and she opened her mouth to say something but then snapped it shut. The scent of her hair filled his lungs, a whiff of lavender, and he took a deep breath, not breaking her gaze.

Bastien's sister.

Only here a week.

Doctor.

He released her arms, and she stumbled back a step.

"Um, here are the sheets." She held them out but then noticed he still had the sweats in his hands. "Oh, you can change in the bathroom. Second door on the left. I'll take care of the couch."

"Thank you. I know it must be weird having some stranger sleep on your couch."

Some stranger who flirted with you at the bar.

Not meeting his eyes, she waved a hand and made her way over to the couch. "Please. A friend of Bastien's is a friend of the family."

Friends. Yes, that's what they'd be. It was all they could be.

"It's funny, though. He doesn't talk about you that much, but when he does, it sounds like you're one of his best friends."

She paused as she tucked the sheet under the couch cushions. "It's kind of odd I never met you before now."

He leaned in and lowered his voice. "Well, technically, we have met."

Her lips pursed and twisted to the side, like she couldn't decide if she wanted to laugh or scold, and her eyes darted to the open living room doorway. "You know what I mean."

He'd been wondering the same thing since he'd walked into her house. Meeting her at the bar without knowing who she was felt like it shouldn't have been possible. Though if he'd met her first as Bash's sister, they probably wouldn't have hit it off the way they had. Jackson would have been extra polite, and she'd have seen him as just one of her brother's friends. She wouldn't have looked at him the way she had in the bar just a few hours ago. Like he was worth her time and attention.

Now that Dr. Miller knew he was just a ballplayer, he didn't expect her to ever look at him that way again.

He leaned against the wall by a window.

"We were only housemates for a year, and there were eight guys living there." The big, old farmhouse had been in a horrible state, but cheap and close to campus. They'd crammed it to the gills with student athletes.

Anais smoothed a pillowcase once, twice, the repeated movement hypnotic to his tired brain. "I didn't visit until graduation. He introduced me and my parents to everyone at the house, but I'd have remembered you." Her cheeks reddened. "I mean, I don't remember you being there."

He clenched the sweats in his hands. The injury in his wrist twinged, and he relaxed his grip. "I was a year above him and then I was drafted my junior year. I've never met any of his family until last year, when I played a game here and I met your dad, and that was only for a quick minute. But he talks about y'all a lot."

This made her smile, and it lit up her tired face. "All good things, I hope?"

"He can't stand any of you."

She laughed, and the already familiar sound wrapped itself around his chest and squeezed.

"You didn't visit until his graduation? California isn't that far." When Jackson had his choice of Division I schools, he'd picked the one furthest from his parents. Bastien had picked the closest.

"I was pre-med." She lifted her chin. "At Georgetown. Finished in three years, like my mom."

He whistled, impressed but not surprised. "And yet you still had time to develop your ice cream and movie matrix?" Anyone who could come up with such a detailed system hadn't been getting Cs in school like he had.

Her cheeks flushed. "That's a recent project."

Dang, she was adorable.

"Was it hard being far from your family? Bastien went home every single break."

Except one, when Jackson had needed him to stay after a terrible fight with his parents. It was a selfless gesture Jackson could never hope to repay.

"Incredibly." A sad, wistful expression dropped over her face.

Everything inside him screamed at him to do whatever it would take to keep her from ever looking like that again.

He cleared his throat. "I'll just . . . go get changed."

Leaving her standing by the couch, he expected her to be gone by the time he got back. He took his time, drank a few handfuls of water, swishing out his mouth, washing his face.

A little tremble went through him when she was still there when he got back. She'd tucked herself into the chair across from the couch with her arms wrapped around her bent knees.

Her gaze was fixed on a window, her eyes taking in the moon through the trees.

"The rain stopped." He plopped down on the couch, holding back a groan at how comfortable it was. Even if he wanted to sleep, the urge to keep talking to her was too strong. "Won't you be tired tomorrow?"

"I got used to surviving on little sleep as a resident." She yawned, rubbing her eyes and then giggled a little.

A jerking shudder ripped through his chest.

"Well, I do need some rest." She tilted her head. "Do you need anything else? Will you be able to sleep on the couch?"

"If I can sleep on a bus full of rowdy, smelly men jacked up on adrenaline after a game, then an oversized sectional is like a cloud."

Another sleepy laugh escaped her. The room was suddenly very hot.

"So baseball, huh?" She leaned back into the armchair. "What team?"

"I play first base for the Weston Wildcats up in Washington."

"Spent any time on the Olympia Ospreys' 40-man roster?"

"A bit." He nodded, once again impressed but not surprised. "You know your baseball."

She waved the compliment away. "My residency was in Seattle. Besides, doctors can like sports too."

A humorless smile pulled at his lips. His parents certainly didn't.

"Do you have ice-cream flavors assigned by teams?"

Her cheeks flushed but she shot him a smirk. "Hot dog toppings."

He laughed. She was unbearably cute. An overwhelming urge to go into details about his injury flooded him. But the last thing he needed was another doctor poking and prodding, giving their thoughts on how he should live his life.

Even if they had excellent taste in ice cream and movies.

She shifted in the chair and tucked her feet underneath her. "Washington must be pretty far from home."

"What do you mean?"

Her eyes went wide and she squirmed, readjusting her feet. "I'm sorry, I just assumed you were from the south because of your accent."

Of course she'd noticed. Her intelligent eyes had probably already spotted his cheap watch and the ratty jacket he'd tossed over the chair in the corner, hallmarks of the pitiful money he made in the minor leagues. At least his shoes were newer.

Arranging his face into what was hopefully a neutral expression, he cleared his throat. "Good ear. I grew up in Charleston."

"Do you miss it?"

"No."

It came out harsher than he'd intended. A part of him was relieved to see the shocked look on her face. If she thought he was a jerk, then it made things a lot easier.

She stood up and rubbed her hand across the edge of her forehead. "I'm sorry. That was super nosy, and you only just met me. Bad habit of small-town doctors, asking too many personal questions immediately after meeting someone."

She'd said something similar at the bar, about asking too many questions. He liked how interested she was in things . . . in him. The reminder of her profession should have put him off, but something about her made him want to tell her more, tell her everything. Except that was the last thing he should be doing.

"No worries." He shot her a smile that he knew women

liked. "It's like you said. Any friend of Bastien's is a friend of the family, right?"

The smile she gave him, however, wasn't the reaction he usually got. It was smaller, sadder than he usually saw. But it was nearly two in the morning. She was probably just tired, like he was.

"Good night, Jackson."

"Good night, Anais."

Despite the exhaustion weighing down his muscles, Jackson didn't fall asleep for a long time.

FOUR

ANAIS

Anais was late and tired and grumpy. Not her favorite way to start the day, but she hoped a quick trip to Carl's Café would sort her out. Isabelle had given her some suggestions on how to approach her dad, but Anais wasn't about to attempt any of them without caffeine.

"Morning, Anais," said Carl Parson Jr. from behind the counter when she walked in. "If you want breakfast, you'll have to wait for a table."

Indeed, the small café was positively bursting with early morning diners sipping coffee and digging into Carl Sr.'s famous donuts. Through the cutout window over his shoulder, she could see various members of the Parson family in the kitchen. The delicious smells of roasting beans, cinnamon, and frying batter hit her nose, and her stomach rumbled.

"No breakfast, but a large black coffee," she held out her thermos, "and a dozen donuts to go would be great."

Isabelle's first suggestion had been to sweeten her dad up —literally.

Carl took the thermos from her and gave her a smile, his eyes crinkling beneath his silvery eyebrows. "Rough night?"

"Bastien." She couldn't say more than that, due to patient privacy and generally not wanting people to know everything about her and her family. Though everyone in town was aware she lived close to the bar and that Bastien would crash at her place after a night out, they didn't need to know all the details. She'd left him and Jackson sleeping that morning, quietly sneaking out the back door of the kitchen rather than through the front door.

"I did hear something about him dancing like a loon last night." He set the coffee down on the counter, and Anais took a grateful sip.

"Oh yeah, from who?"

Carl waved a hand at the round tables behind her, all full of early risers chattering away. "At least three or four women were talking about it. Well, not Bastien, but that friend he had with him."

"Hmm." Anais didn't comment on that, wanting to keep her own thoughts of Jackson Hart to herself. The picture of the same muscles that strained Bastien's old high school sweats being used to dance at Floodline was going to be on her mind all day.

A wistful pang tugged at her heart. Leaning against the counter, she looked around the small room. People were laughing together, people she knew well, people she'd grown up with, people who needed her and her family's medical help on a daily basis. She told herself it was okay that none of them saw her as a potential partner, but the moments of loneliness were getting more frequent.

She couldn't count on someone showing up in town who'd be perfect for her. Even if Jackson hadn't turned out to be Bastien's friend, nothing could come of the spark she'd felt with him. He was a minor league professional athlete, aiming for the money and fame that came with a big contract in a big city.

There was no way he'd ever want to stay in a small town like Jasper Creek.

Look at how miserable Bastien was, after his failed dreams of soccer stardom came crashing down in college. There was a certain kind of person who liked living in Jasper Creek, the kind whose roots went deep, and they never left. Bastien simply wasn't that kind of person, and neither was his friend.

The Parsons, thank goodness, were that kind of people. The delicious smell of cinnamon and bacon pulled Anais's attention back to the counter. She turned, and Carl held out a box.

"Your donuts, doc."

Anais handed over a twenty but Carl waved it away. That happened at least once a week. She rolled her eyes and stuffed it into the tip jar she knew went straight to a college fund for Carlie, Carl's teenage daughter.

"Thanks, Carl."

Anais turned and was heading toward the door when someone called her name. Not breaking her stride, she turned and waved at Isabelle. She was sitting with Tina Page, the owner of Odd Page Books.

Hmm, that's a new development.

Though she'd have loved a chance to stop and chat, Anais was already running late for work. She reached out her hand to open the door, and found herself walking into someone at full speed.

Her coffee thermos tumbled from her hand, the lid popped off, and dark liquid burst out into a Rorschach pattern on the hardwood floor.

"Oh shoot, I'm so sorry." She bent down to pick up her thermos. Not wanting to leave a mess for Carl, she looked around the nearby tables and found a handful of napkins in her line of sight. She snatched them and started wiping.

"I had planned to help, you know. Not just watch," said a

deep, familiar voice above her. Her hand stilled on top of her thermos, and she slowly lifted her eyes.

Peering down at her was Jackson's blue-and-brown gaze.

Anais stood quickly, the last bits of the coffee in her thermos flinging themselves against his shirt.

"Oh no, I'm so sorry." Heat flooded her face when she dabbed at the shirt with the wad of coffee-soaked napkins in her trembling hand.

Well that won't do. She'd sewn up nasty gashes, assisted with surgeries when someone's life was on the line, and her hand hadn't even shaken once.

The mere sight of Jackson had her as giddy as if this had been her fifth coffee of the day, not the first. It wasn't exactly the calm and collected Dr. Miller everyone expected her to be.

"Don't worry about it. It's Bastien's shirt." A mischievous smile spread across Jackson's chiseled face.

Sweet zygoma, the man was gorgeous.

"Can I get you another cup of coffee?"

Aware of the dozens of eyes on her, Anais pulled herself together and stood up straight, a deep breath relaxing some of the tightness in her chest.

"Thanks, but I've got to get to the office." Not that she was looking forward to the confrontation that awaited her.

Besides, more time with him was pointless. At least, that's what her brain was telling her. The swarm of bees that had taken up residence in her chest were telling her something entirely different.

"It won't take long. I already called in an order to pick up breakfast. Bastien said this place has incredible donuts. Caramel with brown sugar custard are his favorites."

His silky smooth voice put three syllables into "caramel," and the bees in Anais's chest buzzed with appreciation.

"I wanted to get some for you too, to thank you, but you'd already left."

"I didn't want to wake you." That didn't sound right. She glanced around the room, hoping no one was listening to their conversation.

Of course, every single eye in the small café was on her and Jackson. Isabelle was practically bouncing out of her seat with curiosity.

"I was sleeping pretty hard."

This set off a burst of chatter in the café that Anais tried her best to ignore. Her phone pinged in her pocket with what she knew would be a text from Isabelle, demanding details.

With a glance around the room, Jackson seemed to finally notice they had an audience. A frown on his face, he plucked the empty thermos from Anais's hand. "Let me go see if my order is ready, and I'll grab you that coffee so you can get to work."

She lingered by the door while he went to the counter, and let out a heavy breath.

In the haze of sleep and panic the night before, he'd been attractive. In the daylight, he was magnificent. Which only made her heart ache more as she reminded herself of the biggest reason that nothing could happen with him.

Even if by some miracle he hadn't classified her as off-limits due to being Bastien's sister, she was headed to Boston in the new year to start a fellowship in women's health. It was at the same hospital her grandad and her dad had done a fellowship. She'd been so proud of carrying on the Miller family tradition, but for some reason her dad was completely against the idea. The fight they'd had when she told him the news made her ache even more than the hypnotizing beauty of Jackson's muscled forearm reaching over to grab a stack of napkins on the counter.

The fellowship would help her take care of both the people

of Jasper Creek and her own lonely single life. Her parents had met in Boston during her dad's fellowship year, and her grandparents had a similar story. She knew it was her chance to finally find love. To find someone who'd want the same things as her and support her dreams the way her dad did for her mom. Even if he made her hands tremble and her pulse race, Jackson had big dreams of his own that had zero room for a small-town doctor like her.

Suddenly he was there in front of her, his hands full of coffee and a takeout bag. The two-toned eyes she couldn't get enough of were framed by wrinkled brows.

He handed her the thermos of coffee.

"Thank you."

She took a sip as his eyes roamed across her face.

"Should we head out? I don't want you to be late for work."

With the weight of dozens of eyes on them, Anais nodded. When he stepped ahead of her so that he could open the door for her, she could almost hear the old ladies of Jasper Creek swoon. Her phone pinged again in her pocket and she turned back to see Isabelle's "you better call me" glare fixed on her.

She gave a polite wave to the room and stepped outside.

Jackson fell into step beside her and they walked past Tina's bookstore and the pharmacy, both closed this early in the morning. "Is it always like that?"

"We don't get many strangers in town. You made quite the impression on people last night."

"Really? Only one made an impression on me."

She glanced at him and caught his eye. As impossible as it was, there was no mistaking the heat in his brown-flecked blue irises.

She turned her head back to the sidewalk. "Thanks for the coffee."

"Thanks for letting me crash on your couch last night."

"Anytime. Though you didn't have to wake up this early. You must be exhausted."

"I'm usually up early to train."

She took a sip of her fresh coffee and closed her eyes briefly. Everything would be easier with caffeine running through her body. Talking to her dad. Walking next to Jackson without drooling.

"I didn't think you'd stick around, not with Bastien's ankle in no shape to hike."

"This trip was as much about hanging out with him as it was seeing the beauty of Colorado."

The way he lingered on the word *beauty* snapped her eyes open. The intensity of his gaze was focused right on Anais and had her hand shaking again. He'd already been responsible for spilling her coffee once that morning, and she wasn't about to let it happen a second time.

Deep breath. At least no one was around to see it if she did drop her thermos again.

"Still, it's a shame to miss seeing it all." She pointed to the mountain that was visible from almost any street in Jasper Creek. "The views from the top are breathtaking."

"Maybe you could show me around instead?"

"Absolutely not."

He chuckled, and heat flooded her face.

Why did I just say no to him?

Her hand slid across her forehead, and she tucked her hair behind her ears. "I mean, I just have a lot to do this week."

Not a total lie. With school out for fall break, countless parents had set up appointments for their kids. Then there was the Halloween festival in a few weeks. The Millers always helped, Bastien most of all. With him injured, Anais would probably have to take on part of his load.

Finally, she had to figure out how to convince her dad to

accept that she was doing the fellowship. Despite all the agitation running into Jackson had caused her already tight-strung nerves, she still had her big plan to talk to her dad. Her emotions had been all over the place since their fight. Her hopes had climbed and fell more in the past twenty-four hours than they had over the course of a month. Until that was settled, she wouldn't be able to think rationally about anything else. The risk of errors would be too high. Things would start to slip through the cracks.

"You're a busy doctor, I get it." Jackson held up the takeout bag. "I reckon I'd better get this to Bastien while it's still hot. And then get him back to his own house."

"Right."

She wanted to ask him what they'd be doing all week, but stopped herself. Whatever they did, it couldn't be with Anais. Bastien lived on the other side of town, and her dad could take care of any follow up on his ankle. There'd be no need to see Jackson, and she shouldn't want to, anyway.

They were in front of the old house with the Miller Family Medical sign in the front yard. "Well, I've got to get to work."

He made a move toward her, past her, and up the stairs. Her heart fluttered at the sight of him holding open the door for her again. With a tight smile, she walked up the steps and into the office.

"Thank you," she said in her most polite, professional voice.

That was who Dr. Miller was. Not someone whose pulse raced walking next to her brother's friend.

But it might be who Anais was.

FIVE

JACKSON

Jackson closed the door behind Anais, telling himself he was being so polite because of the years of decorum drilled into him by nannies, reinforced with stern looks from his mother and aunts. Not because he'd wanted another chance to be close to her.

After all, she'd said no to showing him around town. Clearly, hanging out with a nobody minor leaguer like him was the last thing she'd be interested in. Which was just fine and dandy, since being with a doctor was the last thing he wanted.

With a final look at the clinic's door, he turned away and headed back toward her house where he'd left Bastien with his foot propped up on pillows in front of the TV. The morning sun was warm on his back, and he breathed in the clear air that held more than a hint of autumn crispness. With so much uncertainty on the horizon, he had to remember to appreciate these small moments of calm.

Playing in the Arizona Fall League was a good sign that the Ospreys were finally taking notice of him. He'd been on the 40-man roster for three years, but he'd been optioned back to the minor league Wildcats the entire time. His initial elation at moving up had quickly turned to disappointment that settled in for the long-term.

The current season had been one of his best, however, and Arizona had been the chance to show off everything he'd been working on. His hamate fracture during the second game threw a huge wrench into things. At least he'd played well in the first game, and the surgery had been scheduled quickly.

Despite his aversion to hospitals, he told himself it would be worth it. He just had to be back in shape by spring training if he had any hope of playing in the majors. With no more minor league options left, they either had to put him on the active roster, or put him on waivers. There was no guarantee the Ospreys would keep him, not at his age and not with a wrist injury, even a fixable one. Someone else might, but there was a very real possibility that no team wanted him. It hung heavy over his head, like that last moment you think a fly ball might soar into a home run, but instead hits the back wall and falls into a waiting glove.

The trip to see Bastien was supposed to distract and relax him before the surgery, but instead it was making Jackson realize just how little time he truly had left to achieve his dreams. He couldn't properly enjoy the beautiful Colorado morning he was strolling through, knowing he should have been waking up on a mountain somewhere with Bastien instead. The latest in a long string of injuries was why his friend's MLS career had been over before it started. Jackson hadn't been there to help Bastien during that last disappointing year of college, busy with his second season in the minors.

At least I'm here to help him this week. A small part of the debt he owed his friend could be repaid.

With hiking off the menu, distraction in the form of carbs was what he'd get this morning. Jackson dug into the bag of donuts and bit into one, letting the sugary dough melt in his mouth. There was no stopping the groan that escaped his mouth. A few people passing on the sidewalk gave him a shocked look, but then their eyes caught sight of the bag in his hand and they smiled.

Carl's donuts were apparently an acceptable reason to be making scandalous sounds on the sidewalk in Jasper Creek.

Jackson's phone rang, and he reluctantly put the half-eaten pastry back into the bag. A glance at the name flashing on the screen sent his heart racing. It was his agent.

"Hey, Phil. What's up?" He held his breath. Would it be good news or bad?

"Just checking in."

He let out the breath. *No news was good news*, he reminded himself.

There was a tapping noise, like Phil was typing. "How'd the meeting with the doctor go?"

Though his agent couldn't see him, Jackson made a face. Phil knew him well enough, though, and laughed.

"Hey, I hate hospitals too, buddy."

Jackson bit his tongue. He doubted Phil had years of parental pressure and disappointment hanging over him every time he stepped into one.

His agent kept talking. "But it's important to get this patched up quickly."

"I know."

He could hear the frown in Phil's voice. "Be careful this week. Getting injured again won't help either of us."

It took a lot for Jackson to not roll his eyes at that. He knew Phil genuinely didn't want Jackson getting hurt, but he knew just as well as his agent that a contract with the Ospreys would mean big money for both of them. However, unlike Phil, who worked with a dozen other players, Jackson didn't have any backup plans in case things didn't work out with his baseball career. He knew if he gave himself a way out, he wouldn't put everything he had into it. And he was finally so close after so many years, he could almost taste it.

"I'm not doing anything wild out here."

"That's a relief. You make my job easy, you know. Wish all my players were as well-behaved as you."

Jackson laughed. He was almost to Anais's house. "Uh oh, what happened?" Jackson asked Phil.

He knocked on the front door, then let himself in. Bastien was still on the couch where he'd left him, passed out with golf on the TV. Jackson plopped down next to him and nudged him awake. With a few sleepy blinks, Bastien looked around. His eyes lit up when he saw the bag in Jackson's hands.

"Oh, nothing I can't handle," Phil said with a chuckle in Jackson's ear. "Just promise me you'll never buy a Lamborghini and then race it while drunk."

"That's an easy promise to make."

The signing bonus he'd gotten when he'd been drafted was tucked away in investments, growing slowly but steadily. Almost every other new player had splashed out on some ridiculous car or a house way too big for them.

Most of them had families who could help them pay for things during the season, but Jackson didn't have that luxury. Not since his parents had made it crystal clear he'd be cut off completely if he chose to accept the contract he'd been offered. The choice hadn't been a hard one to make, but it had made the off seasons pretty lean.

Jackson looked at Bastien, digging into his donut with pure pleasure on his face. The winter after Jackson's first season playing for the Wildcats, he'd had nowhere else to go but back to the California farmhouse with his old housemates. It was Bastien who'd been there for him the most. He'd been there that horrible night his parents had come by, offering him one last shot at changing his mind and going back to school, to do the "right thing" and "uphold the Hart tradition." The things they'd said when he'd refused still lived rent-free in his head.

Bastien stayed by his side during the long, miserable days after that night. Not talking, just regular stuff. Sitting with him while he watched TV or played video games. Keeping him busy so he wouldn't wallow in disappointment and misery.

So if that's what his friend needed him to do this week, Jackson was happy to do it.

"My plans this week are fishing and hanging out around town," Jackson reassured Phil.

"Well, enjoy yourself. If I don't have any news for you before then, I'll check in next week when you're back in Arizona. Try to relax. Stay out of trouble."

Bastien must have overheard that last part and raised his eyebrows. A slow grin spread across his cinnamon-dusted cheeks.

Disconnecting the call, Jackson was already shaking his head.

"Oh no, I know that look. Whatever you have planned, it's a bad idea."

"I swear it'll be fun."

Jackson gave him the glare that deserved. "Like how racing last night was supposed to be fun?"

"I usually spend the fall break getting a head start on the Halloween festival preparations." Bastien shifted on the couch. "Would you mind driving me a few places this morning to get supplies?"

The tightness in Jackson's chest released a little. No way they could get into any trouble in a store. "Sure. Sounds great."

• • •

Seven hours later, Jackson was pushing on the same door he'd held open for Anais that morning. The large reception room had a few people in it, and a young brunette behind the check-in desk. She looked too much like Anais, with a touch of Bastien around the nose, to be anyone other than one of their younger siblings. It really was Miller Family Medical, just like the sign outside said.

"Hi, I'm here to pick up a prescription for Bastien Miller."

The young woman behind the counter looked him up and down, then smiled back at him. It was open, friendly, but not entirely trusting. "Let me go check with the doctors."

She stood up and hurried off through the door to the left of the room. There was another door on the right, and it opened, revealing a nurse with a clipboard, who called one of the older ladies sitting in a chair by the wide windows overlooking the lawn.

Jackson gave a small smile to the women remaining, their curious eyes fixed on him. Rather than sit in one of the empty chairs set in groups of four around the room, he leaned against the counter, facing away from everyone.

He'd spent the entire day running Bastien from one store to the next, searching for the perfect shade of orange paint. The back of the truck was filled with plywood, strings of purple lights, and empty metal pails. But when they were unloading everything, Bash's ankle had started throbbing, and he'd called his dad.

Somehow, Jackson had gone from not setting foot in a doctor's office for ten years, to being in them twice in one week. Apparently, there were no limits to what he was willing to do for his friend.

He glanced back at the women behind him, all still peering at him over the top of their magazines, and tightened his fists.

The movement made his wrist ache, and he turned back quickly so they wouldn't see the grimace of pain on his face.

"What are you doing here? Are you okay?"

Jackson looked up at the sound of Anais's voice behind the counter. The late-afternoon light streaming in from the windows hit her dark hair, turning some strands more golden, others a warm honey.

If they'd been back at the bar that first night, he might have given into the urge to tell the pretty girl sitting next to him about his hand injury and upcoming surgery. With Dr. Anais Miller, he held it in check. There was nothing she could do that he hadn't already done for himself.

"I'm fine. Bash called your dad when his ankle started hurting worse. I'm here to get his prescription."

It was the opposite of what Jackson would have done. His parents were the last people he thought of when he wasn't feeling well.

Anais frowned. "We don't have it here. He would have called it in to the pharmacy. Did you go there?"

Of course it wouldn't be here. He shook his head, his pulse racing at the realization he'd made himself look like an idiot in front of Anais. She ran a hand along her hairline, her brows furrowed. Earlier, when she'd said she had too much work to show him around, he thought it was a polite brushoff. But the pinched look on her face and distraction in her eyes spoke to an overwhelm that was real. A surge of protectiveness rolled over him, a desire to help that he only felt with a select few people in his life, Bastien being one of them.

It's just because she's Bash's sister, he reasoned.

"I'll just give them a call." She turned on her heel and headed back into the hallway, leaving Jackson alone with the receptionist. There was a heavy pause while she looked at him, her dark eyes dancing with questions. The corners of his lips lifted.

"Hi, I'm Jackson, Bastien's friend from college."

"I know." There was a pink tinge to her cheeks, and she looked down at the desk, rearranging some papers. She was clearly shyer than her older siblings, and she reminded him of his little sister, Madison. "I'm Clementine."

She said it the French way, *Clemen-teen*, not the southern way. Jackson's family had stuck to the president's names: his sister was Madison, his father was Jefferson, and his uncle—also a doctor, of course—was Ford. It seemed the Millers had their own traditions. He'd have to ask Bastien if his family was French or if his parents just liked the way the names sounded.

"Nice to meet you, Clementine." He gave her a wide smile, and the pink tinge deepened. "How long have you been working here with your family?"

"About a year." The papers lay still, and her fingers moved to the keyboard in front of an ancient-looking desktop computer, her eyes still not meeting his. "I finished my undergrad at Centennial U last year. I'm working here while I apply to medical schools."

"Another doctor in the family, huh?"

Her lips thinned. "That's what Millers do."

"Bastien's not a doctor," Jackson said.

She lifted one of her shoulders and continued to tap away at the computer. "Every family's got a rebel."

"I guess that's why we're friends. My whole family is doctors, too, except me."

She finally lifted her eyes to look at him, and they were wide with surprise. "Really? They weren't mad?"

Jackson laughed. "Furious. But no one's mad at your brother, are they?"

Clementine rolled her eyes. "Yeah, well, he was always good

at sports, even when he was little. It wasn't really that big of a surprise when he wanted to be an athlete instead of a doctor. Besides, there was always Anais."

The tone she used to say her big sister's name was how Jan Brady said "Marcia." Jackson coughed, hiding another laugh.

"What about me?" Anais walked back into the room. She looked at Jackson and said, "Bastien's medicine should be ready in half an hour." Then she narrowed her gaze at her sister.

Clementine's eyes darted around in panic, finally landing on the papers under her hands and shifting them around again.

"I was just asking when your last appointment is." It was the first thing he could think of to take her attention off Clementine. It had nothing to do with his ongoing and pointless desire to spend time with Anais.

Anais's eyes narrowed. "Why?"

Disappointment rippled through his stomach. This morning's brushoff wasn't a one-time thing, it seemed. Hoping his face looked indifferent, he shrugged. "Bastien is bored. I thought he might like to see some family instead of my ugly mug."

She turned to her sister. "Minnie, what's the rest of the day look like?"

Clementine tapped a few keys on the keyboard in front of her. "You have appointments until six." She shot an apologetic look at Jackson before giving a sheepish smile to her sister. "You told me to fit in Matt Hayes after he called you this morning."

A familiar mix of jealousy and anger roiled in Jackson's stomach. Of course she'd put other people before family. That's what doctors did.

"Maybe tomorrow then." Jackson turned to leave. "I need to go get that medicine for Bastien."

"I know a bored Bastien isn't fun." Raising an eyebrow, she flashed him a half-smile, and his anger disappeared instantly. "I'm sure you can handle him on your own for one evening."

Oh, that was true enough. But could he handle what the other Miller twin was doing to his head? He hadn't been this unsettled since the first time he'd walked into spring training. Once he was focused on a goal, he stuck to it, no matter what.

The decision to forget about Anais didn't seem to want to stick, however.

You'll be gone in a few days, he reminded himself as he stepped out of the office and into the crisp October air. As far as he knew, there wouldn't be another chance to see Anais. Out of sight, out of mind had worked before.

No reason it wouldn't work this time too.

ANAIS

Weekly game night at the Miller house was starting off strangely, and not just because her dad was avoiding her. He'd run off before she could even say hello, claiming her youngest brother, Elias, needed help with his AP bio homework.

Her attempts to talk through things at the office yesterday hadn't been possible, thanks to unexpected appointments and house calls. The donuts hadn't gone to waste, of course. She'd eaten most of them after Jackson had showed up at the office and flustered her in the way only he seemed to.

Not one to give up on a goal, she tried again to talk to her dad at work, but it had been just as busy as the day before. She was determined to have it out before they started the game tonight. Except now she was distracted by the extra plates set on the dining room table.

"Is Danielle here tonight?" Her youngest sister lived on campus at her school in Fort Collins, and would sometimes come home unannounced—usually when her fridge was empty and her laundry hamper was full. Seeing her youngest sister more often was one of the things she'd been looking forward to most when she came back to Jackson Creek.

Her mom shook her head. "Bastien and Jackson are coming, of course." She pulled out silverware and handed it to her.

Anais clutched the forks and knives in her hands and stared at her mother, abandoning all thoughts of laying the silverware down next to the plates at perfect right angles the way she always did.

"Why?'" Her heart pounded in her ears.

"They're not out hiking. What else do you think Bastien would do tonight?"

Her stomach lurched and embarrassment trickled through her veins, icy hot in her blood and surely turning her face red. Luckily, her mom wouldn't notice the change in her coloring as instantly as her dad would.

Naturally, that was the moment he finally decided to walk in.

"Sweetheart, are you ok?" Her dad's mouth turned down and his eyes scrunched up behind his glasses. "Not coming down with anything, are you?"

Before she could answer, he was already on the other side of the table, hands reaching out to cup her cheeks. Not even their ongoing fight could keep him from worrying about her. She sighed but opened her mouth obligingly, knowing it would be quicker to just let him check than to argue. It was wonderful working with her father, after growing up wanting to be a doctor just like him, but there were some disadvantages. Like every sniffle and shiver setting off both his doctor and fatherly instincts.

Her mother was the opposite. She worked at CUH, Centennial University Hospital, and dealt with complicated cases every day, leading teams of residents and interns running on just a few hours of sleep. As long as Anais could stand and wasn't throwing up, Dr. Heather Miller considered her fit to work.

Dr. James Miller III, however, would have her in bed with a blanket over her lap every other week.

"I'm fine, Dad," she said. He brought his hands to her neck, feeling her lymph nodes. "I was just up late the other night with Bastien."

Her mom tsked loudly from the kitchen. "I still can't believe he walked all the way from the bar to your house on an injured ankle."

"He didn't do it on his own. Jackson helped him."

"Oh yes, Jackson." Her dad smiled.

"You know him?"

"I saw him play a few times when his team was in town to play the Grizzlies. Bastien introduced us after the game once."

Anais frowned. Where had she been?

Oh right, medical school, then residency. Where Bastien would have been, too, if he hadn't loved sports more than medicine.

If only sports had loved him back. The ankle injury in his junior year of college was the reason he was hurting so much from a simple stumble down the stairs. It was such a shame. All that wasted talent because of some bad luck when diving for the ball.

It had been hard enough to see her brother disappointed. Anais couldn't imagine the life of an athlete's wife, handling broken dreams and missed opportunities on a regular basis.

Heat flooded her chest as Jackson invaded her thoughts yet again. She looked down at the silverware in her hands and started lining it up next to the plates. If all it took was a few minutes of flirting for her to picture herself married to someone, she was lonelier than she realized.

"Have you been to many games with Bastien?"

"I go as often as I can." He took a pile of napkins from the sideboard and set them neatly in the middle of the plates. There was a heavy pause, as if he was considering how to phrase something. "You can come, too, now that you're home."

Anais's fingers stilled in her adjustment of a fork. "You mean once I'm home after my fellowship."

There was a sharp inhale from her dad, and total silence from her mom in the kitchen. Anais set her shoulders and looked up. Her dad's mouth twisted down.

It was ridiculous. They'd always agreed on everything, and in the rare cases when they hadn't, her dad had been more than willing to listen. Even when she was a ten-year-old explaining why it would be better to eat ice cream before dinner to ensure she was getting adequate calcium, given her dislike of broccoli.

In this situation, however, he refused to see reason. Anais kept her voice calm, like she was talking to an upset patient. "You and Mom both did a fellowship after residency. Grandad did one too. At the same hospital."

"That doesn't mean you have to." His voice was just as calm. Calmer, even. She tried not to get jealous. He had thirty more years of practice, after all. "You just got back a few months ago. It's wonderful having you home." His eyes met hers. "We missed you so much when you were gone. I just want more time with you here, working beside you at the office."

Familiar guilt and longing tore at her heart. She'd gone to Georgetown for college, then Seattle for medical school and her residency. After over a decade away, it was wonderful to be home, and not just because of the superior donuts. Working with her dad was what she'd always dreamed of.

"You know I love it here, Dad, but I can't wait too long, or a fellowship won't be in the cards for me anymore." There was the simple fact that most programs wouldn't consider someone with too many years as a practicing physician. It was just too hard to start over, to unlearn your way of doing things and get used to taking orders again from attendings again. "If we want to stay in business, we need more specialization."

Her dad's fellowship had been in geriatric medicine, which was great, but the population of Jasper Creek was getting younger, not older, as more families moved in. People were more willing to go further to get the care they needed all in one place than they'd been when he'd started practicing medicine three decades ago.

Her dad waved his hand holding a napkin, like he was shooing away a pesky insect. "A few years won't make that much of a difference."

He was probably right, but she wasn't about to admit that. Time for another tactic. "You seem to be forgetting I'm a woman and can't have kids in my forties the way you did."

"You're not even thirty. You have time." Her dad refolded the napkin and placed it on a plate. "And you don't need to have five like we did."

"Before I have any, I need to actually meet someone to have them with."

"There are plenty of nice men here in Jasper Creek."

Instead of replying right away, Anais remembered Isabelle's advice and inhaled slowly through her nose.

The simple fact was that Anais wanted a family, though maybe not quite as big as hers. She loved her siblings, but five was a lot of kids. Following in her mom's footsteps of an unexpected pregnancy with twins at twenty-two during her first year of medical school had never been Anais's plan. The plan was to meet someone in medical school or residency. Or, since that hadn't happened, during her fellowship.

While she knew her dad was right that twenty-eight was nowhere near an age to get concerned about not being able to have kids, she also wanted to find someone to love, to share her life with. The fear that she never would grew with every passing year. All her careful planning was not yielding the expected results.

She folded her arms across her chest and raised an eyebrow. "I think our definition of 'nice men' might differ a little."

Sure, she'd had dates and even a few exclusive, boyfriend-type relationships during college and medical school. But once she shared her plans for joining her family's medical practice in a small town, men drifted away, their interest waning. There was never an explicit conversation about it, but there were always not-so-subtle hints from the men she'd dated that Anais was expected to give up her dreams to follow theirs.

It was the last thing Anais could ever see herself doing, even if life would be so much easier if she could. And it was all her parents' fault.

There was no one more in love than her parents, and no two people were happier in their chosen careers. They'd met when her dad, broken-hearted after being dumped by his girlfriend in Jasper Creek, had done a fellowship in Boston where her mother was pre-med. Their unbearably romantic story had set the bar high for the Miller siblings, in both love and work.

The fellowship in Boston was the key. It's where her father had met her mother, where her grandfather had met her grandmother. That's where Millers met their soulmates. Not in Jasper Creek.

Jackson clearly didn't count, even as a shiver of anticipation crept down her spine at the thought of seeing him tonight. If he'd been staying around longer than a few days, and had been anything other than her brother's professional-athlete best friend, Anais would have been in trouble. Lucky for her, he'd be gone by the end of the week, and she'd be off to her fellowship and her future.

Before she or her dad could say anything else, there was a

knock at the door. Without waiting for someone to answer, Bastien let himself in.

"The fun has arrived," he proclaimed loudly, moving the crutch under his arm with the ease of someone who used it at least once a year. Jackson was right behind him.

"Thank you for having me over, Dr. Miller," he said to her dad, who shook Jackson's hand before heading into the kitchen.

With just those eight exceedingly polite words, Jackson had set Anais's stomach churning. Ten minutes had hardly been enough warning for her body to prepare for seeing him again. Combined with the lingering adrenaline of the unfinished fight with her dad, she had to put a hand on the table to steady herself as he drew near.

"Can I help you with that?"

Jackson's words sent a zing of electricity through her. It was getting worse, she realized. That couldn't be normal, or healthy. If she hadn't studied the human body for so many years, she might think it was just being tired or sick.

But no, it was him. It didn't take a doctor to notice how gorgeous he was, and her reaction was perfectly normal. Though by the fourth exposure, she should have started to build up some sort of immunity.

"I've got it, thanks." She brushed the hair from her forehead and his eyes followed the movement. A warm heat forced its way into her face, and she turned, adjusting a few forks that were slightly crooked.

Bastien hobbled over on his crutch, and they both turned to him. "I'm so glad it's game night. I've been super bored."

Jackson raised an eyebrow. "Bored? When I've been running you around town like a chicken with its head cut off?" He placed a hand dramatically on his chest and twisted his face in mock offense.

Bastien rolled his eyes, but Anais's lips turned up in a smile.

"Speaking of chickens with their heads cut off." Their mother appeared at the table with a bowl of salad that she laid on the table to point a finger at Bastien. "You need to take it easy."

"Says the woman who had five children and was chief radiology resident by the age of thirty-two."

"I had help." She turned to beam at their father, who had just walked into the dining room. Ten years older than his wife, his hair was already gray at the temples, the laugh lines deep around his mouth and eyes. He was frowning, however, as he put his arm around her shoulders and looked at his oldest son.

"I have help too." Bastien gestured around the table. "You all help me. Jackson is here helping me."

"You know that's not what I mean." Her mom glared at her brother in a way Anais was sure sent interns under her direction trembling. "You do everything in this town. Teacher, coach, event planner . . . next thing you know, you'll tell me you got licensed online to perform marriages and will be doing that for the tourists that pass through in the summer."

"Well, now that you mention it . . . " His smirk fell away at the look on his mom's face.

"Your mother's right." Their dad's soft voice was gentler than their mom's, but still stern, like he was talking to a patient with a recent cardiological event who was refusing to stick to a healthy diet. "It's one thing to be finding your path after not being able to play soccer, but if you keep going at this pace, your ankle will be the least of your worries."

"Oh, I don't believe this. One little slip down Floodline's broken stairs and suddenly I need to completely change my life?"

This could take a while.

Shaking her head, Anais caught Jackson's eye and tilted her head toward the kitchen. "Help me with the rest of the food?"

The pensive look on his face smoothed out, and he followed her out of the room, anticipation flickering through every part of her body.

Jackson's nerves had been rattling since Bash had told him about family game night. Offering to drop him off and then not stay would have raised too many questions. Now he was given the opportunity to be alone with Anais, the one thing he'd been hoping to avoid.

He followed her into the kitchen without a second thought.

"Sorry about that," Anais said as she opened the fridge to grab a bottle of wine. "Family game night usually starts with appetizers, not a lecture for Bastien."

"Don't apologize. They really care about him."

She turned her head, her eyes full of concern and curiosity.

Dammit, I must have sounded sad.

"Of course they care. We all do." Clearly knowing the layout of the familiar space by heart, Anais put the wine down and reached up to grab glasses from the shelf above the counter without taking her eyes off Jackson. "That's why it drives me up the wall how reckless he can be."

Crossing his arms over his chest, Jackson raised an eyebrow. "Racing down some stairs is reckless?"

"No, it's not just that." She sighed and leaned against the

counter, a hand at her hairline. His fingers itched to brush aside the invisible strands for her. "He'll go super hard for months, then take a week to blow off some steam. Rinse and repeat. It's not good for him."

"Or his hair." The weak attempt at a joke burst out of Jackson before he could stop it. Feeling awkward in a way he never was around women, he shifted his gaze to a corkboard full of photos hanging on a closed door. They were all of the Millers doing various outdoor activities or on vacation together. Everyone was laughing, happy, hugging.

When he looked back at Anais, a small smile spread across her face. She poured two glasses and offered him one. Their fingers brushed when he took it from her, and he thought he heard her inhale sharply. His pulse ticked up.

Jackson took a sip of wine. "It was like that in college too. A week of all-nighters to study for finals, then a massive party when it was all over. Hours in the gym and at practice, then lying in bed an entire day playing video games." His lips turned down. "I didn't realize he was still like that."

"It wasn't that bad when he was with—"

"Brenda?" Jackson asked, and Anais nodded. "Oh yeah, he told me all about her."

Again, a surprised look crossed Anais's face. "You must be really close then. He doesn't tell many people about her."

"Maybe because I don't live nearby, it was easier to talk to me." Sending support via texts about the slow deterioration of Bash's relationship with his long-term girlfriend had been almost a second job all last season.

He took a sip of wine and changed the subject. "Have any favorites from that big bookshelf out there?"

Anais raised an eyebrow, then she gave a little nod, like she approved of him not wanting to talk too much about her brother's past relationship. Gossip wasn't his thing. It was his parents' thing, part of the world he'd left behind.

"Oh sure." A dangerously sweet smile danced across her lips. "Though I'm more of a movie person, really."

His heart gave a little stutter. "So I've heard."

A beat passed, and their eyes met. That same playful tension they'd had in the bar sizzled in the air. Anais opened her mouth, but before she could say anything, Clementine popped her head in.

"We need another chair for the table." She eyed the door with all the pictures on it, then looked at her older sister. "Could you run down and get one?"

Anais gave her a glare. "Were you sent to deliver a message or to get it yourself?"

"Would you rather hand out the game's mystery envelopes to make sure Bastien doesn't cheat?"

Anais groaned and turned to Jackson, gesturing to the door behind him. "Excuse me."

He stepped aside, opening the door as he did, revealing a staircase that must lead to a basement.

"Oh, and don't forget, I won't be at the office tomorrow. I have an interview."

"Medical school?" Jackson asked.

Anais paused at the door next to Jackson. The smell of lavender invaded the air as she turned to him. "She's applied to all the same ones I did." The pride beaming from Anais's face made her eyes sparkle.

Clementine, however, seemed a little uncomfortable with all that approval aimed at her. Her jerky nod seemed even more nervous and shy than she had the previous day. She grabbed the bottle of wine from the counter, and shifted it from one hand to the other as Anais made her way down the stairs.

When her sister was gone, Clementine opened her mouth as if she wanted to say something, but closed it with a snap and hurried out of the kitchen. The similarity to his sister, Madison, struck him so strongly, he almost pulled out his phone to call her.

"Minnie? Are you still up there?" Anais's voice floated up from the basement. "I need your help."

Jackson set his glass on the counter and headed downstairs.

"I don't know why Dad put them up on top of—" She gasped when she turned to see him standing by the stairs.

The basement was finished, the floor covered in worn, beige carpet and the paneled wood walls peppered in colorful stickers at knee-height every few feet. What must have been a playroom when the Miller siblings were little had become a mix of TV room and storage. Anais was in front of an open closet, staring up at the top shelf stuffed with stacked folding chairs.

"Need help?" Jackson stepped around a worn couch to stand next to her. He took a deep breath and lavender filled his nose again. Beside him, she shifted, and her arm brushed against his.

Technically they'd been alone in the kitchen, but the murmur of voices and noises from the dining room were completely gone in the quiet of the carpeted basement. It felt like they were the only two people in the house.

"I can't quite reach." Anais's voice was a hoarse whisper that sent prickles of sensation up his arms. Her eyes flitted between his eyes and his mouth. She licked her lips. "I was going to ask Minnie to bring down a stool—"

"I've got it." Holding her gaze, he reached up with his uninjured hand and grabbed hold of a chair. When he brought it down between them he took a step closer. "Here you go."

She licked her lips again and stepped forward to take it. "Thanks."

They were as close together as they could be, with only the

chair separating them. Jackson hadn't let it go yet, and his hands were right next to hers. Her ragged breaths whispered across his skin as he struggled to keep his own breathing normal.

A thousand thoughts were competing for space in his head. Some of them were telling him to step back, go upstairs, and behave himself. The rest were all reminding him that if he moved his hand just a few inches, he'd be touching her, the way he'd wanted to that night at the bar. Before he'd found out she was Bash's doctor sister.

Just as he started to sort out his thoughts and decide one way or another, Anais surged forward and pressed her lips to his.

The electric zing that shot through him lasted barely long enough for his scattered brain to register what was happening. There were too many things he wanted to do—bring a hand up to her neck to pull her in tighter, run his fingers through her hair, wrap an arm around her waist—but he never got a chance to even fully consider them. She pulled away almost immediately, her face the bright red of a sunburn.

"I'm sorry, that was—" She let go of the chair and her hands flew up to her forehead. "Not what I'd planned to do."

It was hard not to laugh at that. "Had you planned to do something else with me down here?" He raised his eyebrows.

"Stop it." She wacked his arm, which only made him laugh harder. "I don't know why I did that."

"Maybe because you've been thinking about it since the other night, just like I have?"

Of course he'd been thinking about it. He'd been doing everything he could to not think about it, which meant he'd been thinking about it twice as much. It was Anais who had actually done something about it. He was tempted to ask if she had a sweet treat assigned to every kind of kiss there was. This had to be something like a Girl Scout cookie. Delicious but brief, always leaving you wanting more.

"Maybe." She frowned. "Well, now that it's happened, we've gotten it out of our systems, right?"

There was a hitch in his chest, a warning tightness like right before he slid into a base a half-second too late.

"Pardon?"

Her eyes were looking everywhere except his, and her fingers were playing with a strand of her hair. His fingers itched to do the same. Instead, he clenched his hands tighter on the chair.

"I mean, we've both been thinking about it since that night, but then couldn't once we found out I'm Bastien's—I mean, you're his—"

She closed her eyes briefly and took a breath. The centering move was familiar, one Jackson had used countless times during games. When she spoke again, her voice had lost its wavering, uncertain quality. She was all business, more serious than he'd ever seen her, even at the doctor's office.

"Nothing can happen between us." Her eyes met his, full of a familiar cool logic he hated. "But we both needed to see what it would be like."

"*We* did, huh?" The chair was digging into his palms, his wrist screaming in protest. He shouldn't have been surprised that she was like this. What doctor didn't think they knew best for everyone?

Then, just like a doctor, she ignored his words and acted like he hadn't spoken. "Now that it's happened, we can move past it. Pretend it never happened."

The crushing realization hit him harder than a fastball to the chest. She was embarrassed. Doctors didn't want ballplayers, as his parents had pointed out years ago. They certainly didn't want minor league nobodies. Add on to that he was her brother's friend, and of course she'd want to forget this ever happened.

"Certainly." The word was short, polite, and laced with as much subtle snobbery as his southern upbringing could manage.

Her lips turned down a little, but then she nodded. He was surprised she didn't want to shake his hand and make this little exchange something official.

"Thank you for your help with the chair." She turned on her heel and marched up the stairs without looking back.

The feeling of dismissal was familiar, and shouldn't have stung as much as it did. He tried to remind himself that this was a good thing. He hadn't wanted to feel anything for her, for lots of reasons. It was only his stubborn streak that wanted something even more the second someone told him he couldn't have it. That same streak had gotten him this far in his career, and it would take him even further next year. It had to. Then everyone who didn't think he was good enough would feel as stupid as he did right now.

Dinner would be awkward as all get out, but he'd gotten through worse growing up.

He took a few moments to calm himself, then headed back upstairs, thanking his lucky mitt that he'd be leaving Jasper Creek in a few days.

EIGHT
JACKSON

It was déjà vu for Jackson, standing in front of Anais's house, with a limping Bastien hanging off him.

The expression on Anais's face when she opened the door was familiar too—surprised, exhausted, irritated, and underneath all that, worried sick about her brother.

At least it wasn't raining.

The plan tonight hadn't been to go out, but to watch the first game of the World Series at home with Bastien. Then Jackson had gotten the call that his surgery was postponed. So close on the heels of Anais's rejection, the news that his major league dreams were slipping even further out of his grasp meant the last thing he needed was a night of watching others play the game he loved.

Bash, being Bash, had taken the mood-lifting mission too far and now here they were again at his sister's doorstep.

She looked tired, and so beautiful it made Jackson's chest hurt. There was a moment of hesitation when she caught Jackson's eye. Her gaze lowered and lingered for just a brief second on his lips before she shook her head a little, ran a hand over her forehead, and focused on her brother.

"What did he do this time?" She stepped aside and Jackson helped Bastien into the hallway. Between the small entryway and the size of the two men, she couldn't back up that much, and her arm brushed against Jackson's. Their eyes locked. He caught a whiff of lavender and the memory of their kiss overwhelmed him.

The very small part of his brain still working properly reminded him that he was holding his friend who was heavier than sin—and also Anais's brother. It wouldn't help anything to drop him in the middle of the hallway.

"I was arm wrestling with Carter Hayes." Bash bent his head to his arm that was tucked against his chest, a rag full of ice clutched to his shoulder.

Two bright pink spots appeared on Anais's cheeks and her eyes flashed. She looked ready to lay into Bastien, but then turned her eyes to Jackson.

"How is it possible he's injured himself twice since you've been in town?"

"Hey now, I'm not his babysitter."

Her anger caught him off guard. He should just drop Bastien in the hall and let her drag him into the bedroom.

Friggin' know-it-all doctors ruining my life.

Before he could talk himself into actually doing it, she slammed open the door to the guest room and stomped inside.

Once he'd laid Bastien on the bed, he turned to leave but found Anais blocking the door, her arms folded tightly against her chest and her eyes flashing. Even madder than a wet hen, she was gorgeous, which made him even madder. Mostly at himself, for noticing.

"You're his friend, and he's an important part of this town. All anyone will be talking about for weeks will be your visit and everything that happened."

There was a tightness in his chest that a deep breath didn't ease. Up until then, the Millers had appeared to be the opposite of everything he knew about medical professionals. They hadn't seemed selfish, or worried about status or money the way all of his parents' friends were back in Charleston.

But they must have just been putting on a nice face for Bastien's friend. Everyone had their secrets, their mean streaks. The more he thought back on their interactions, the more he realized that Anais was a little too concerned with people in town seeing her in a positive way. She'd been almost trembling with worry that people in the café would overhear them, more concerned about the spilled coffee on the floor than the person she'd bumped into. Even that first night she'd been like a tour guide, making sure he experienced the best of Jasper Creek. Wasn't much different from his parents wanting to look good in front of their rich friends.

That must be the real reason nothing could happen between them. She didn't want anyone seeing them together.

"If people want to talk, I reckon that's their business, not mine." His voice was dangerously low.

Bastien piped up from behind him on the bed. "Nissy, it's fine. He's been a good friend this week."

Anais ignored her brother, still staring down Jackson. "Does being a good friend back in Charleston mean challenging him to races and egging him on in fights he's sure to lose?"

"Maybe."

A deep wound opened up inside Jackson's chest. His expression must have been as dark as his mind, because Anais took a step back. Then her face softened and her arms dropped to her sides.

"I'm sorry. I know it's not your fault that Bastien's so hard-headed."

The apology threw him off balance. He'd been warming up

for a fight, and wasn't quite sure what to say now. He settled for a grunt of agreement.

"My hard head is sitting right here." Bash waved from the bed with his good hand.

Anais pointed a finger at him. "And you'll stay there while I figure out a bandage. I haven't had a chance to replace the one I used to wrap your ankle."

She stormed out of the room, leaving Jackson with Bastien, who was giving him a strange look.

"What?" Jackson's stomach gave a lurch, sure he was about to get chewed out for his rudeness. If he ever heard anyone talk to Madison the way he just had to Anais, he'd tan their hide.

"Are you sure you have to leave tomorrow?"

He blinked, not expecting that. The Miller twins were keeping him off balance tonight. "I mean, I technically don't have to. Not now that the surgery's been pushed."

His surgeon had gotten hurt playing golf and they had to reschedule. The irony of an orthopedic surgeon with a sports injury would have been funny if it didn't put Jackson in serious danger of not being able to play in the spring. He didn't really need another reason to dislike doctors, but ruining his last chance at a career in the majors was now pretty high on the list. The hospital said they'd call back in a few days, and Jackson hadn't heard from the team yet if he should fly back to Arizona or not. There must be a surgeon there he could use, but he was dreading dealing with even more doctors to find a new one. Besides, the guy in Denver was supposed to be one of the best in the country. Though apparently the worst at golf.

Bastien gestured to his injured foot and shoulder. "I can't do much right now, and there's a lot the town needs."

"Like what?"

"Like booths for the Halloween festival."

It took a moment for the request hidden in that statement to make its way to Jackson's brain. He took a step back, shaking his head.

"Oh no. Absolutely not."

"Why not? I could pay you."

Jackson shot him the look that deserved. "It's not about the money."

Right on cue, his wrist gave a twinge. The risk was too high, and too much depended on him having his best season ever. That meant recovering from this fracture. If he couldn't get the surgery, he'd have to keep it immobilized for at least six weeks, which would cut into his winter training time. This wasn't the time for climbing ladders and wielding power tools.

He leaned against the wall and crossed his arms. "My hand's not in much better shape than yours."

Bastien rubbed his good hand over his face. "I know, it's just . . . " He leaned back on the bed and sighed. "I basically run the Halloween festival and there's no way I can do that now."

"And I can?" His heart was pounding. Driving Bastien around picking up supplies was one thing. But this kind of event organization was well beyond his abilities. Everything was, really. He knew how to swing a bat and catch a ball. That was it. That's all he had to build his future on. Whatever he'd learned in the handful of semesters he'd been at school before being drafted had long been forgotten.

"Calm down. I'd still be there to make sure things go okay. I just can't do any of the physical stuff." He waved a hand before Jackson could point out neither could he. "I'm not talking about heavy lifting. You've seen all the running around we did this week? It's mostly that kind of stuff."

Jackson blew out a breath. "You don't have a co-organizer or something?"

"Nope, it's always just me." Bastien shrugged and his lips turned up. "I can be a bit hard-headed apparently."

Jackson was in no mood to smile back. "I'm sure there's someone else you could ask. Literally anybody else."

Bastien grew quiet. "Maybe, but . . . I'm asking you. Please."

That one word froze Jackson's next protest in his chest like ice. The two friends had been there for each other without question over the years, but neither had resorted to the P-word more than a few times.

The two men stared silently at each other, and this was the scene Anais walked back into. She hesitated in the doorway.

"Uh, you two okay?" She approached the bed. "Bastien, you look like Hart stole your cookies-and-cream sundae or something."

The use of his last name stung in an unexpected way.

"Something like that," Bastien grumbled and held out his arm for his sister to wrap it. "Jackson won't stay to help me with the Halloween festival."

Her eyes flicked to his, and he pushed away the heat that coursed through him. If he was staying, it was for Bastien, not to spend more time with his sister. She'd made her feelings about him crystal clear.

"Maybe he has to get back to training," Anais said, pulling the bandage around her brother's wrist.

Bastien winced. "He can train here."

"Maybe he has plants he needs to water."

"He can buy new plants. I can't buy a new ankle."

"Maybe he—"

"Maybe he wants to speak for himself?" Jackson's voice was low again, and two pairs of eyes shot his way. Bastien's were pleading, Anais's were . . . hard to tell, but they were full of fire. He'd been burned enough in his life to know that staying away was safer.

But he couldn't just leave his friend, not when he was hurt. Not when Jackson did—despite what he'd told Anais—feel slightly responsible for this new injury. He'd put money on Bash losing the arm wrestling fight, which had likely spurred him to push extra hard.

Jackson rubbed his hand across the back of his neck. "How big of a deal is this Harvest Halloween spectacular thing?"

"It's the major event of the year. Brings in a lot of money for the town."

Jackson groaned. Of course Bastien would have signed on to run something that big on his own.

Anais looked up from wrapping Bastien's shoulder, her eyes suddenly softer. "I'll probably help Elias with the baseball team's milk bottle game."

No surprise she'd be involved in some way. The town was small enough, everyone probably pitched in for the event. There was no way his presence was as necessary as Bastien thought it was, just like his role in organizing it probably didn't have to be solo. An extra pair of hands would be helpful, but there was no way to know if the proximity to Anais would be too much for him.

A glance at her eyes revealed a heat in them that seemed less angry than before. His breath hitched. Did she want him to stay, despite what she'd said after the kiss?

"As long as I can have a few hours per day, and you can find me a real gym for training, I can stay another few weeks." He wouldn't overdo it on his arms, but he could still do cardio and lower body.

Bastien whooped from the bed and stuck his arms in the air. Not quite done wrapping his wrist, Anais clicked her tongue impatiently. The bandage had completely unraveled.

"You'll have to buy me some Rocky Road too, Bash," Jackson said.

Anais's eyes met his. Something silent and dangerous passed between them.

Oh yeah, she definitely wanted him to stay.

And he definitely shouldn't be so happy about that.

It was still the early weeks of flu season in Jasper Creek, but if the past few days were any indication, it was going to be a long one.

Anais held back a sigh as she looked over Clementine's shoulder at the packed schedule for the day, and then out at the waiting room that didn't have a single empty chair.

Despite having ordered the vaccines as usual, they'd been late arriving. Not all of their patients had made the effort to go to the nearest hospital thirty miles away to one of the flu shot clinics.

This could have been preventable, if her dad wasn't so stubborn. Normally she admired that he stuck to his convictions and kept doing things the way the Millers always had, but his resistance to change meant they were faced with a waiting room full of people coughing and sneezing, waiting their turn for a test to confirm it was really the flu, and for something that would ease the symptoms.

If I can't change his mind about things, maybe Austin can.

The only bright spot in what was starting off a rough day would be the planned visit from Dr. Austin Gibson, her friend from residency and potential replacement when she left for her fellowship. Austin worked at CUH and knew her mom. The plan today had been to have him come for lunch, spend some time with her dad, and see the office. It was as much about convincing Austin to come as it was a campaign to reassure her dad—and Anais if she was being totally honest—that things would be fine while she was gone.

But the packed waiting room meant her plans were in tatters. There was no point in Austin even coming if all they'd have was twenty minutes between appointments to eat at her desk.

Anais walked back into the hallway and found her dad in the break room, pouring himself his second cup of coffee that morning from the machine on the counter. The small room wasn't fancy, with just a coffee machine, microwave, and mini fridge to stock the leftovers from family game night. The cabinets mostly held extra medical supplies. The tiny table in the middle of the room barely had space for two people. The three Millers and the two NPs who worked with them usually took turns eating lunch.

Her dad held the mug out to her. "Here. We're going to need extra energy today."

Anais frowned but took the coffee. "We wouldn't have had this problem if we were part of the hospital group."

Leaning back against the counter, her dad shook his head. "No, it would have been worse, because the delays are every-where, and we'd have been last on their list to get a supply."

She should have let it drop, but the unfinished fight from family game night had left Anais feeling unsettled all weekend. Then there was the fact that Jackson Hart was still in town, which shouldn't be bothering her. That kiss was supposed to get him out of her system. What other option did she have? Fall for a guy who was the total opposite of what she wanted and who she had no possible future with? Overall, it had been a long, grumpy few days hiding in her house rewatching *The Witcher*.

The glower she sent her dad's way would have made Geralt of Rivia proud. "Why can't we at least meet with them?"

"When the practice is yours, you can do what you think is best." He gave her a small, proud smile. "And you'll do a great job when that time comes."

The smile was a peace offering, but wasted on her current mood. Even so, she couldn't stop her chest swelling with emotion. At least he was trying. She should take it easy on him.

Or, she could keep pushing, like the fifteen straight hours of Henry Cavill had convinced her was a good idea.

She raised her eyebrows. "Don't pretend it won't be at least another ten years before you retire."

He rubbed a hand across his face in a move that reminded her of Bastien. "I might consider stepping back sooner if you weren't going away for the fellowship."

So that was his angle . . .

Irritation flickered in her veins. Anais set her coffee down on the table and folded her arms. "You're serious? If I don't take the fellowship, you'll join the hospital group?"

It wasn't her first choice of how to keep their practice relevant, but she couldn't ignore the advantages of being part of a larger medical network. Even if people preferred to see the Millers for most things, including flu shots, that didn't mean they weren't losing patients. There were more specialists in surrounding larger towns, and it was often easier for people to have all their doctors in the same place.

The other option was her fellowship. It was a way for Anais to specialize that would help the people of Jasper Creek and help keep Miller Family Medical around for the next generation.

It also might be her last shot at love.

Her dad raised an eyebrow. "I won't join immediately, but I'll take a meeting, like you've been asking since the day you got home."

She blew out a frustrated breath. Not even eight-thirty in the morning, and she was already exhausted.

"Not good enough. We have more to gain by me leaving than we do by me staying."

"We have a lot to gain by you staying."

Unbidden, thoughts of family game nights and lazy weekends binging TV with her sisters and Isabelle filled her mind. She pushed them away.

"Millers always do a fellowship in Boston." And they always found love there. Who was she to mess with generations of a winning formula?

"It will still be there in a few years." His eyes softened. "It's so nice to finally have you here to help. And not just at the office. Your brother overextending himself is really starting to concern me and your mother."

Thinking of Bastien, of course, made her think of Jackson. Which soured her mood again.

Rather than continue the pointless back and forth, she grabbed her coffee and wished him luck for the day before heading back into the hall and into her office. The stack of reports on her desk would have to wait until she'd seen all her patients, but the coffee was needed now.

The knowledge that Jackson was still in town was more unsettling than the dozens of sick residents waiting to be treated. At least with the flu, she could prescribe a course of treatment she knew could help. What prescription could she write for the state she was in over the blue-and-brown-eyed mass of muscles who would now be around for another few weeks?

Steam bath with anti-embarrassment essential oils to

dislodge the rude words thrown in his face. She hadn't meant to be so short with him, but she'd just been so worried about Bastien. And fine, she'd also been exhausted.

Take two memory-wiping pills to forget that kiss ever happened. The one kiss should have gotten things out of her system, like she'd told Jackson . . . but that was when she thought he was leaving. Since he was staying, more kissing would be possible.

One large glass of nerve tonic before the next encounter. Like that was something she could predict. She could hide over the weekend, but she couldn't during the week. With her luck, he'd show up in the office, coughing and feverish.

Maybe she'd tell Austin to come anyway. She could ask Isabelle to bring something from the bar and eat with them. Twenty minutes with friends in the middle of a busy day would help her feel better, even if it didn't change her dad's mind about anything or get Jackson out of her head.

Comforted to have a new plan and her coffee mug empty, she hurried to her first patient. She might not be able to solve all her problems right now, but she still had an important job to do. Dr. Miller couldn't be stressed or worried, or the whole town would be. She had to pretend like everything was fine. Eventually, it would be.

Anais was just finishing up with Mrs. Foster when there was a knock at the exam room door.

Clementine poked her head in. "Nissy, there's someone to see you."

Holding back a sigh, Anais widened her eyes and gestured at the older woman sitting on the table.

"Oh, sorry, I thought you were all done." Her sister flushed. "Dr. Miller, you have a visitor."

"It's fine, dear, I've known you both since you were in diapers," Mrs. Foster said, quite unhelpfully, as Minnie shut the door. "You're the third generation of Dr. Miller who's taken care of me."

"I know." Anais's heart filled with pride at the thought. "Are we doing a good job?"

"Of course. It's not your fault I got sick. I just hope I didn't pass it on to your Aunt Deb."

"You saw her this week?" Anais's aunt didn't come into town much, preferring the quiet of her farm. Since her dad had been one of six kids, Anais could understand the desire for some solitude. After all, she'd just spent a much-needed forty-eight hours avoiding her entire family. Aunt Deb also had a few social anxieties, but either friends or family came to see her a few times a week at least.

"Last Thursday, I think it was." Mrs. Foster considered for a moment. "I wasn't feeling too poorly then, so I'm sure she's fine."

Anais made a mental note to check with her dad if anyone from the family had been out to see her over the past weekend. Getting the flu at her age could be dangerous.

"You'll be fine, too, as long as you keep resting, and take those over-the-counter meds. I wrote them all down for you." She handed the older woman a piece of paper.

"Thank you, Anais, I will."

Anais said goodbye and practically sprinted down the hall to her office. Happy relief flooded her when she opened the door to see both Isabelle and Austin waiting for her with three greasy takeout bags from the Floodline on her desk.

"Oh, I'm so glad to see you."

Austin's bright blue eyes twinkled under his dark eyebrows. "Are you talking to me or the cheeseburger?"

"The cheeseburger, of course." She bent down as if to give him a hug, instead reaching out to swipe a bag off the desk.

He laughed, and Isabelle shot Anais a familiar questioning look. Isabelle had met him a few times before, when the two friends had gone to Denver for a night out. The question of why Anais and Austin had never been an item was one Isabelle had been asking since she'd first laid eyes on him.

Yes, Austin was extremely handsome, but he was almost too handsome, if that was possible. Even worse—he knew just how attractive he was. With most people, he turned on the charm to eleven, and got pretty much whatever he wanted.

Maybe it was because she'd grown up with Bastien, but Anais had had zero patience for Austin's smug swagger the first day of residency. She'd put him in his place quickly, correctly answering the attending's question that he'd gotten wrong, all while subtly insulting his peacock preening.

What had the potential to become an epic rivalry had quickly turned into a solid friendship, however, when they'd both been stood up for a date at the same bar. Between his shock at the thought that someone didn't want him, and Anais's proof that no one would ever want her, they'd finished an entire bottle of tequila and spent the next miserable day vomiting up their terrible choices at her apartment. Nobody had ever heard about that night, Isabelle included.

Anais gave an exaggerated hug to Isabelle before sitting down, and Austin stuck his tongue out at her.

"What did Isabelle bring for you?"

Austin sent a wide smile her way. "A salad. It looks absolutely delicious."

Isabelle fluttered her eyebrows and fanned herself. "So many charming men in Jasper Creek this week. I don't know what to do with myself."

The burger Anais had just bit into caught in her throat.

Would Austin ask what other charming men Isabelle was referring to?

No, Austin only heard the compliment to himself, thank goodness. Sometimes his gigantic ego made her life easier.

They made quick work of their meals while Anais caught Austin up on what had happened at last week's family game night. She left out the kiss with Jackson, of course. In fact, she left him out of the story completely. If Anais didn't talk about it, it would prove that the kiss had done its work and Jackson was out of her system.

Not talking about it didn't keep her mind from lingering on the way his lips had felt pressed against hers, however . . . or the way he'd looked at her when he'd brought Bastien over the other night.

"Why don't I just go say hi to your dad now?" Austin said, putting down his empty salad bowl. "You don't have to tell him you want me to replace you next year."

"I mean, I'll have to tell him eventually. He does own the practice." Anais popped a fry into her mouth. "But are you sure it's what you want?"

"I just submitted the paperwork to leave my position." Austin's lips turned down. He hadn't shared the full story of why he was so eager to leave CUH as soon as possible. The reason he'd given her was that he didn't want to work in a large hospital anymore. But Anais knew there had to be more to it than that. She suspected his playboy reputation had gotten him into trouble, but wouldn't press for details.

After all, she didn't exactly feel like sharing the details of her romantic failures at the moment.

"I'll let you go do that. I need to head back to the bar." Isabelle grabbed her purse and headed out with a wave.

Austin rubbed his hands together. "Into the lion's den we go."

Anais ran a hand over her forehead, pushing away any stray strands of hair. Her stomach churned. This had been her original plan. It would work. It had to work. If her dad got excited about Austin being there to help in her place, then he'd stop pressuring her to stay. Then she could go to her fellowship, forget all about her brother's handsome ballplayer friend, and meet someone perfect for her.

They went into the hall and down a few doors to her dad's office. The door was closed, and Anais knocked, her hand only trembling a little, not enough for Austin to notice.

When the door opened, it wasn't her dad on the other side, however.

It was Jackson.

TEN

JACKSON

Jackson opened the door of Dr. Miller's office and ice filled his lungs.

There was something he instantly disliked about the tall, dark-haired man standing there with Anais. Maybe it was the smile, full of perfectly straight white teeth. Maybe it was how familiar he looked, the way he reminded Jackson of every guy he went to high school with, all perfectly coiffed hair and smug attitudes.

Maybe it was because Anais was holding on to his arm.

"Jackson." Anais's eyes were wide, but she didn't remove her hand from the guy's bicep. "What are you doing here?"

"He was dropping off something from Bastien." Dr. Miller came out from behind his desk.

That was only partially true. Jackson had been interrupted by the knock on the door just as he was about to ask Dr. Miller about other orthopedic surgeons in the area. Now he felt a surge of relief that he wouldn't have to get into the details of his injury with yet another doctor. It was for the best that he'd been interrupted from asking for help he wasn't sure he actually needed.

Even if that interruption did have a very punchable face.

"Hi, Dad." Anais turned to the smiling buffoon at her side. "Look who came for a visit."

Jackson stepped aside so Dr. Miller could shake hands. "Nice to see you again, Austin."

The two men shared a warm greeting, then he stuck out his hand in Jackson's direction. "Hi. Dr. Austin Gibson."

Of course he's a doctor.

It was ironic that Jackson was surrounded by them, yet none of them could help him. The league had their own doctors, but he hadn't been able to get ahold of anyone this week. Phil still didn't have news from the team about if they wanted him to stay or not. With no chance of him playing any of the fall league games, Jackson had to show them he'd be ready in time for spring.

He was even willing to dip into his savings to pay for the surgery himself if he had to, though it made his chest tighten to think of touching the money that was supposed to be for Madison. His sister deserved a chance at the life she wanted, and he was in a position to give it to her. Well, he would be once he made it to the majors. And to do that, he needed his fracture taken care of.

The ice in Jackson's lungs hardened to steel as he shook Austin's hand.

"Jackson Hart." He shortened and flattened out the A in his last name. Then, for good measure, he added, "First baseman for the Weston Wildcats."

Austin nodded, his expression completely unreadable. "Friend of Bastien's?"

"Best friend." Jackson's eyes darted to Anais, then down to where her body was touching Austin's. With a start, she quickly drew back her hand. Something inside Jackson's chest unclenched a little.

Anais met his eyes. "Austin's a friend from residency."

What kind of friend was what Jackson wanted to know.

"Do you have a minute for me, Dr. Miller?" Austin flashed a perfect smile at Anais's father.

Dr. Miller checked his computer screen. "Looks like my next patient is late, so I have some time."

Jackson stepped back to let Austin enter the small office, then made his way out into the hall. To his immense pleasure, Anais didn't follow her friend, but stayed next to Jackson.

"I'll just go grab a donut while you two chat," Anais said to her dad, then she turned to Jackson. "Would you like one as well?"

The words were perfectly cordial, as if nothing had ever happened between them. It almost made him want to say no, but then he caught Austin glancing between the two of them.

"That'd be great, thanks." He flashed his own version of Austin's sparkling smile at Anais, and was rewarded with a rosy flush of her cheeks.

Austin frowned but closed the door. A burst of triumph shot through Jackson's chest, until he turned to see Anais glaring at him.

"Was that really necessary?"

He blinked, feigning ignorance. "I don't know what you mean."

She rolled her eyes and walked down the hall. "Come on, I'll get you some coffee."

He followed her without saying anything. He was being childish, and he knew it, but this kind of jealousy was new for him. The look she'd given him the other night was burned into his brain. She wanted him, he was sure of it. That's why she'd insisted Jackson and Bastien not stay at her house the way they had when Bash had hurt his ankle. Being around Jackson had to have the same effect on Anais as being around her had on him.

She led him into a small break room where nearly every

surface was covered in photos of the Millers, holiday cards, and birth announcements. Some looked to be from decades ago. The office overall was updated, but the history was still there. The Millers had been doctors in Jasper Creek for a long time.

That should have cooled whatever heat was thrumming through him, a reminder of why she wasn't right for him. Then she turned her head and a whiff of lavender reached his nose and his shoulders dropped, all tension leaving his body now that he was alone with her.

"You're like Bastien," she said. With the same familiarity she'd shown in her parents' house, she pulled out mugs without looking at what she was doing. "Coffee?"

He nodded. "You mean because we're both incredibly good looking?"

That got a small chuckle and another eye roll. "You can't turn off the competitiveness, can you?" She poured a cup from the urn on the counter and held it out to him.

He grinned. "It's what makes me such a good ballplayer."

Even without the stats to prove it, he knew he was good. The potential to be great was there, if someone would take a chance on him. Except taking a chance on a twenty-nine-year-old with a broken hand wasn't as easy for teams as it was to scoop up eager twenty-year-olds.

"It's what got Bastien hurt." She reached for a familiar brown bag on the small table at the center of the room, pulled out a donut, then held out the bag to him. "I'm surprised it hasn't gotten you hurt yet."

The opening was there to tell her about his hand, why he'd been in her father's office. He held back, though, that same competitive streak not willing to admit she was right.

"Baseball is physically demanding, sure, but it's really the most mentally challenging sport."

"I'm not sure Bastien would agree." She bit into her donut

and briefly closed her eyes as pure pleasure swept across her face.

Reaching into the bag for a donut of his own, Jackson chuckled at both her expression and at what she'd said about Bastien. It was an argument he'd had often with his friend.

"Bastien's never had to deal with the long, slow pace of a game where you spend most of your time standing still and swimming in your own anxious thoughts." He took a bite from his donut and let out an audible moan. "Why is all the food in this town so amazing?"

Anais giggled. "There may also be a competitive streak in our town. The Hayes who own the Floodline, and the Parsons who own Carl's Café have always tried to outdo each other."

"The Millers, the Hayes, the Parsons." Jackson shook his head. "Is everything in this town a family business?"

"Is that a bad thing?"

If she'd been upset or insulted or asked with anything other than true curiosity, Jackson might not have answered. But her eyes were open and sincere and looking at him the way she had that night at the bar. Like it mattered what he thought.

"It's just . . . not what I'm used to."

"I can't picture Charleston as full of chain stores and mega-marts." She munched on more of her donut.

He took a sip of coffee and cleared his throat, his eyes drawn to the flecks of cinnamon sugar dusting her lips. "The families I know don't seem to like each other the way you all do here."

"We don't like each other all the time."

"Even some of the time is miles better than what I had."

Her eyebrows drew together, and he inhaled sharply.

Too personal.

He set his coffee on the table and brushed the sugar off his hands. "I mean, you might be competitive here with your food, but it's nothing compared to what I've seen southern families do with politeness."

A smile fluttered at the edge of her mouth.

"Does that come in handy in baseball?"

He chuckled. "Only if you're a Rockford Peach."

There was a sparkle in her eye. His heart gave a little leap, pleased she'd recognized the reference to *A League of Their Own*.

"I never got a chance to ask you how you liked the ice cream."

"It was incredible."

Instead of answering, she licked her lips slowly, the last of the cinnamon disappearing under her tongue. The same sizzling tension that filled the air in the basement was zinging around the tiny breakroom. Jackson's breath caught in his throat and he took a step forward. He could hear her breath catch in her throat in a tiny gasp.

He lowered his voice and leaned in close. "Are you sure that kiss got me out of your system the way you thought it did?" He kept his gaze steady as he waited for an answer, pushing down the fear that she'd rebuff him yet again. What was one more rejection from a doctor when he'd grown up hearing how little he'd be worth if he wasn't one?

"Maybe one was an insufficient sample size."

His heart pounded in his ears and she licked her lips. They were inches apart now, so close he could see the individual sugar crystals sprinkled across her mouth and cheek. He reached up to brush a few away, and her eyes flooded with heat.

"I will be here a little longer, if you're interested in further experiments."

"That would be . . . " Her raspy voice trailed off and she took a tiny step back. She tilted her head, considering. "Would you really be okay with that?"

"With being an experiment?" He pictured a chart ranking kisses and their effects on her, similar to the one she must have for ice cream and movies. The idea that Austin might be on that chart sent a surge of hot jealousy through him.

"Yes, well, no, not like that." Her cheeks flushed. "But clearly there's something interesting to explore here. It could just be something fun, while you're here. If you'd want to?"

Fun? Yes, he could do that. It's what Phil had recommended while he waited for another surgery appointment. *Be patient, have fun.*

"I like fun." He smiled and could feel her pulse quicken under his hand. "I do play a game for a living."

A meager living, but that didn't matter. Anais just wanted to be his vacation fling. She wasn't thinking of him as a potential partner, and that was totally fine. There was nothing else he could offer her, and he wasn't about to say no to the possibility of more kisses with a smart, gorgeous woman.

"We wouldn't tell Bastien, obviously."

"Obviously." A fling wasn't anything for his friend to get worried about. Bash didn't want Jackson to hurt Anais, and that clearly wouldn't be possible in this situation. She'd set the limits around what it was, and Jackson wouldn't do anything she didn't want to.

"Great." She stuck out her hand, and he chuckled as he shook it. "I look forward to our future collaboration."

As if he'd known Jackson had just slid into a victory worth crowing about, Austin popped his head into the break room.

"Hey there. All done with your dad."

Anais turned to him and blinked, then gave the other man a smile.

"How did it go?"

"He seemed to really like the idea of me working here."

Squealing, Anais dropped Jackson's hand, jumped forward

and wrapped her arms around Austin. Meanwhile, Jackson's heart hammered in his head, his pulse an ocean pounding in his ears.

Slowly, he took a deep breath. This was what he trained for. The slow buildup of tension followed by elation with disappointment chasing right behind. He was used to adrenaline flowing through his veins with no immediate way to release it. He was a master of his emotions. The last thing he wanted was for Dr. Austin Gibson to see how much the interruption had bothered him.

Jackson cleared his throat. "I've got to get back to Bastien." He gave Austin the kind of polite smile that he'd seen his mother give the women she hated the most back in Charleston. Then he winked at Anais and flashed his wide grin again. "Thanks for the coffee and donut. I'll see you real soon, Anais."

Anais looked up at him, her cheeks flushed. "Soon."

He gave a nod to Austin, who barely returned it, his eyes dark and narrowed.

Out in the crisp Colorado sunshine, a smile spread across Jackson's face as the day stretched before him. It didn't matter if Austin would be working with Anais. Jackson would be the one having fun with her while he figured out how to get his surgery.

ELEVEN
ANAIS

"I like that Dr. Gibson."

Every evening, once all the patients were gone and the paperwork was filed, Anais, her dad, and Clementine all congregated around the reception desk. The two NPs had already left, so it was just the Millers talking through their days.

Anais leaned against the desk, trying to remain casual. "What did you like about him?"

Her dad shot her a look. Her act hadn't fooled him for a second. "His experience in emergency medicine, of course."

"A fellowship is a very valuable thing, it seems." Anais kept her face blank.

Sighing, her dad shook his head. "He's leaving before he finishes though. Because he realized it wasn't for him."

Anais blew out a breath and crossed her arms. "You don't have to worry about that with me. I finish what I start."

Just like she was doing with whatever was happening with Jackson. If one heart-melting kiss wasn't enough to convince her brain that he wasn't an option, then she would simply make another plan. This was a new situation for her, which meant more data had to be collected. Maybe it would take five kisses to get him out of her system, or ten, or just one more. She couldn't know for sure until she tried.

"Is that a bad thing?" Clementine said, swinging back and forth in her chair in front of the turned off computer. "To change your mind once you're already on a set path?"

"Not necessarily." Their dad scratched at the rough gray stubble on his chin. He looked tired, and Anais made a mental note to ask Minnie to shift some of his patients to her for the week. "I think there's probably more to the story than he told me today. I'll have to ask your mom if she's heard anything at the hospital about why he might be looking to leave early."

Anais had been thinking the same thing. She'd rather hear it from Austin himself, but her mom might know more about the politics of it all.

"It'll be nice to have someone new here," Minnie said.

There was a twinkle in their dad's eye. "You mean someone young and handsome?"

Minnie's cheeks flushed pink. "Jackson's way more handsome. Don't you think so, Anais?"

It was a blatant attempt to dig for information, but Anais had more practice at this than her younger sister.

"They are both physically attractive in their own ways." Her voice was calm, with just a hint of retribution. Minnie's face paled.

"Well, I'll let the two of you sort that out among yourselves. I need to get home and start dinner for your mom." He gave them both a kiss on the cheek before heading out.

As soon as he was out the door, Clementine stood and grabbed her own coat. "I don't know why he bothers when Mom is totally the better cook."

"It's sweet, that's why." Anais pulled on her coat. "She has a long commute every day, so it's nice for her to come home to dinner on the table."

Clementine made a face so disgusted, Anais had to laugh. "You're the only one who ever complained. The rest of us eat whatever he makes. You're the picky one, Minnie."

She held her nose in the air. "It's not my fault I have refined taste." Her eyes darted to Anais. "Probably why I prefer Jackson's looks to Austin's."

Anais leveled her best big-sister glare at her. "Neither of them is an option. For either of us."

Red burst across Minnie's cheeks, her words sputtering. "I didn't mean for me. They're so—and I'm so—"

Her shyness around men was almost legendary, and Anais didn't take her teasing any further. If Clementine didn't date much, it was just one less thing for Anais to worry about. It was already stressful enough to think about what her youngest sister, Danielle, was getting up to while away at college. Though she was pre-med, like Anais and Clementine had been, her grades weren't great.

At least she could stop worrying about Jackson. Her plan to just have fun with him meant she wouldn't be so anxious every time she saw him. Her nerves would settle again, and she could focus on smoothing things out with her dad. Today had been a good start. Austin had unlocked the door for her.

Now it was up to her to figure out how to fling it all the way open and make her dad see how the fellowship was the best thing for everyone. Anais followed Clementine out of the office and into the hazy twilight, breathing in the crisp Colorado air she'd missed so much while she was away. It helped clear her mind like nothing else could, and she had to come up with a new plan of attack to finish what she'd started.

The next few days were so busy with flu patients, Anais barely had time to eat, let alone have any fun with Jackson or think about a new plan for her dad.

She tried to focus on the positive: the talk between Austin and her dad had gone well. It was a relief to have one thing she could put from her mind, at least until the week was over.

Just as soon as one thing was checked off, however, something new was added.

"I'm worried about Aunt Deb." Her dad stuck his head into her office, where Anais was shoving a sandwich in her mouth in the ten minutes she had between patients today.

"Why?"

"No one's seen her in town for almost a week, according to the last three patients I saw this morning." Her dad's lips were twisted down, throwing his deeply etched worry lines into stark relief.

A shudder ran through Anais. It was easy to forget how old he was most days, especially with her mom ten years younger than him.

If he was getting old, her dad's eighty-year-old aunt was definitely old. She lived alone on a farm that didn't always get the best cell reception. Despite the family begging for years for her to come live closer, she said she liked the quiet. It was even quieter now that her husband had passed. Her dad's cousins had moved away years ago.

"Who's the last person who went out to the farm?"

"Mrs. Foster. Last week." Her dad ran a hand across his face. "She said she'd been coughing and blowing her nose."

There was only one Mrs. Foster in town and Anais had just seen her that week to test for the flu. It was more than likely Aunt Deb was just as sick, if not worse.

"I called her three times, and she didn't pick up." Clementine had just appeared next to her dad at Anais's door. "Should I call the sheriff to go out?"

Anais shook her head. "We already know she's likely sick, so I should just go now."

"I can go," her dad said, but Anais had already stood up and put on her jacket. He looked twice as tired as she felt.

"You did the last house call, I can do this one."

Her sister had already started back down the hallway. "I'll work out the schedule for the rest of the day, move anyone I can to tomorrow." It would still be a busy day for her dad at the office, but he'd have the NPs and Clementine to help him. The long, bumpy ride out to the farm, then dealing with whatever state Aunt Deb was in, would wear him out much more than it would Anais.

"Thanks, Minnie."

Anais rushed to grab the home visit bag from the supply closet, then headed out of the office, trying not to let any of her anxiety show on her face to the patients still waiting in reception. Once outside, she pulled out her keys, but slowed to a stop when she noticed the slight lean of her car to one side.

The front right tire was flat.

Her esophagus tightened. "Great."

There are always options, she reminded herself. *Just work through them logically.*

Her father usually biked to the office when it was nice, and so did Minnie. The twenty-minute bike ride for one of them to get their car would add a ton of time to the trip.

An hour wouldn't make that big of a difference, she told herself. Except now that she was so worried about Aunt Deb, putting it off any longer than necessary just ratcheted up her anxiety by a thousand.

She took a deep breath and considered her other options.

The two NPs lived within walking distance of the office, so

they were one-car households, and their spouses used the cars for their jobs in another town.

There were countless people who'd be willing to give her a ride, so all she had to do was figure out which one would be the quickest.

At this time of day, Basiten would be two streets away at town hall, working on Halloween festival business. She pulled out her phone and leaned against her inaccessible car. She'd have to call Avery down at the garage as well to take care of the flat, but that could wait until after she was sure that Aunt Deb was okay.

When her brother picked up the phone, she didn't even bother with hello. "Bash, I need a ride. No one's seen or heard from Aunt Deb in days, and we're worried she might have the flu."

"I'd love to help, but I can't drive, remember? Doctor's orders."

She groaned. In her panic to get to her aunt, she'd totally forgotten.

"Jackson is here with me. He can drive you wherever you need to go."

Her stomach gave an involuntary jump. This wasn't what she'd had in mind when they'd agreed to have some fun while he was in town. "You're just volunteering him for everything now, huh? The Halloween festival, now chauffeur. Is he going to be bat boy at the game this weekend too?"

Bastien laughed. "I'm working on the bat boy thing."

"Didn't he drive you to town hall? How will you get home?"

"I can get a ride with someone else."

As much as she didn't want to admit it, Jackson was probably the best solution she had on such short notice. Any shimmering excitement about seeing him was smothered in worry for Aunt Deb.

"How soon can he get here?"

"He just walked out the door, so he should be there in about two minutes."

"Thanks, Bash."

"Don't thank me, thank Jackson when he gets there."

She disconnected the call and checked the time. Two minutes gave her enough time to run back inside and grab a few more supplies for her bag.

And a donut for Jackson.

When he pulled into the parking lot, she was waiting with her bag in hand, and she didn't even let him turn off the engine before opening the door and hopping in.

"Thank you for this." She held out the donut, her hand shaking a bit with what she told herself was just worry. It was definitely not from being so close to Jackson for the first time after they'd made their agreement. "I'm sorry this is the opposite of fun."

"It's no problem." He placed the donut on the console between the seats and reached over to squeeze her hand. "I hope your aunt is okay."

Helping seemed to be his default, but this burst of sweetness was unexpected and set her heart pounding against her rib cage in a dangerously erratic rhythm.

"I'm kind of grateful for the break, actually. Bastien and the other volunteers were getting weirdly heated in their discussion about orange versus purple lights."

Despite the tension throbbing in her veins, Anais giggled. "That happens every year. And Bastien always loses."

Jackson made a three-point turn in the parking lot and faced the main road. "I reckon he's in the right. Purple is way spookier."

Anais smiled and her shoulders relaxed a little. What would have been a lonely, stressful ride was, thanks to a flat tire and

Jackson's easy charm, smoothing away the rough edges of her worry.

His eyebrows raised above his multicolored eyes. "Now, where're we headed?"

The light moment was over. Anais directed him out of the parking lot and down Main Street. Aunt Deb lived outside town limits, down an unpaved road that led into the woods surrounding Jasper Creek.

Five minutes passed without any sound other than Anais giving instructions.

"I'm sorry, by the way," he blurted out after they'd made the next turn.

"For what?" Had he done something horrible in the two days since she'd last seen him?

Jackson's eyes flicked to hers. "For waking you up the other night. You seemed crankier than a drunk raccoon in a corn maze when we showed up for the second time in a week."

She chuckled at the vivid image he painted. "You did wake me up from a pretty nice dream."

"Oh?"

She flushed, but didn't give any details. He didn't need to know that Jackson had replaced Henry Cavill in her crime-solving dreams. "Take the next right."

His eyes turned back to the road and he followed her instructions. "She's really isolated out here. Did she always live so far from town?"

"It wasn't that bad when she had her husband and kids." With a sigh, Anais ran her hand along her hairline, brushing away a few wayward strands. "Her husband died last year, but none of my cousins wanted to take over the farm and all moved away."

"Millers actually moved away from Jasper Creek?" His lips turned up. "Hard to imagine."

"Calm down. They only moved to Aspen and started a ski school." Anais paused. "Besides, they're technically Walkers."

"Still. Another family business."

Her eyes slid over his face, trying to read his expression. There was something deeply mistrusting about him, whenever family or certain medical topics came up. "Well yeah. If you can't trust your family, who can you trust?"

He was silent for a moment. "No one goes to check on her?"

"We do, but she's pretty independent. She's usually in town every day for coffee or food or to visit someone. That's why it's concerning that no one has seen her in a few days."

"She doesn't have a phone?"

"Reception isn't great out there and we had a storm last week, so it may be even worse than usual. Clementine called her earlier and no luck."

"It's really great that you're all so worried about her." There was a sad sort of smile on his face.

"Your parents aren't worried about you playing professional sports?"

Now his smile twisted into a frown. Anais felt a pang of regret. She thought she'd been encouraging, but should have known from experience with Bastien how sensitive athletes could be.

"I'm sorry, I just meant—"

"It's fine." He glanced over at her and gave her a quick smile that set her pulse racing again. "I'm just a little stressed, waiting on a call from my agent this week."

"That's right, the World Series ends soon. Are you a free agent?"

He raised his eyebrow at her, curiosity painting his face. She squirmed in her seat. All week, she'd been too tired to do anything once she got home other than turn on a favorite movie and scroll on her phone. If that scrolling had taken her to a few

—or a dozen—articles about minor league baseball rules and contracts, that was just a coincidence.

He squeezed his hand on the steering wheel and a muscle tensed in his jaw. "Things are still up in the air for next season."

It took everything in her not to ask the questions bouncing around in her head. Despite the hours of research, she'd only learned the basics, not the details. She'd also drawn the line at looking him up directly. That felt like cheating her way into knowing him.

This was the perfect time to get answers, if she could figure out a nonchalant way to ask her questions. How long were contracts usually for? Did they base it on past performance? What were his stats last year? Were any teams in Colorado interested in him?

That last one was because she was thinking of Bastien, obviously. He'd been thrilled to have his friend so close. She'd be in Boston next year.

Before she could ask anything, however, the sign for the Walker Family Farm appeared.

"Take a left up ahead."

She had to stay focused. This thing with Jackson was temporary. They'd both agreed to that. An interest in his job was normal, but planning for an impossible future was just torturing herself.

Besides, once she took care of Aunt Deb, she still had to figure out how to convince her dad to be okay with her leaving for the fellowship. That was the only way to get the future she actually wanted.

TWELVE

JACKSON

Anais was nervous, he could tell. A slightly shaking hand knocked on the door. Fingers ran along the edge of her forehead. Her bottom lip pulled under her teeth. They were the signs he'd looked for when playing against Bastien—sports, card games, anything competitive—to give him the advantage.

With Anais, those same nervous gestures created a hot bloom of concern right in the middle of his chest. He rubbed at it, in what he thought was a discrete way, but then Anais's eagle eyes flicked to the movement.

"Are you okay? You didn't train too hard this morning, did you?"

He dropped his hands at his side. "I'm fine. Focus on your aunt."

Anais frowned and looked back at the closed door. "She's not answering." She looked around. "Her truck is here."

Jackson took a step forward and pounded on the door with a closed fist. "Mrs. Walker?" Anais cringed slightly next to him. It was his booming locker-room voice, the one he used to be heard over everyone all amped up before a game.

From inside the house, there was a quiet sound of shuffling feet.

"I heard you the first time, goodness gracious. No need to knock down my door."

Beside him, Anais let out a sigh that sounded as relieved as Jackson felt. He fought the urge to put his arm around her to give her a comforting hug. That's not what she wanted from him, or what he wanted to give.

Head in the game, Hart.

The door opened and a small, white-haired woman wrapped in a crocheted blanket peered up at them. "Oh, Anais, I thought it might be you." Her gaze shifted to Jackson. "Is this the ballplayer everyone's been drooling over?"

Despite the tense situation, Jackson let out a small burst of a chuckle. "Hello, ma'am, I'm Jackson Hart. People have been pretty worried about you, Anais especially."

"Don't know why." She coughed, a tiny one, almost like clearing her throat. "I didn't want to bother you for a little cold. I didn't grow up with a doctor for a father without learning the basics of what to do when I'm sick. I'd have been one, too, if I'd been born twenty years later."

She stepped aside and waved them in, mumbling under her breath. "Instead my blockhead brothers got medical degrees . . . would've poisoned half the town if I hadn't stepped in . . . "

Jackson caught Anais's eye as they followed Aunt Deb inside, and she rolled her eyes like this was typical behavior for the old lady. Fighting against a grin, he realized that even if she lived outside of town and had married a Walker, Aunt Deb was still very much a Miller.

She led them into a warm, cozy living room that was messier than the house he'd shared with Bastien in college. Mugs littered every surface, and piles of books teetered at the ends of couch cushions. It looked like a tissue factory had exploded all over the floor.

Beside him, Anais let out a frustrated huff and immediately reached into her pocket for a protective glove. With a snap of latex, she put it on and bent to pick up the tissues right in front of her. "Didn't want to bother us? Aunt Deb, this is why—"

The old woman held up her hand. "If you've come to lecture me about moving closer to town, you can stop right there. A messy room doesn't mean I can't take care of myself."

It would have been a great speech, except then she started to cough, bent over double with the violence of it. In a flash, Anais had stuffed the tissues into Jackson's hands and hurried over to rub her aunt's back. After a solid minute of no end in sight for the coughing, Jackson wandered away to find a trash can for the tissues and a sink to wash his hands.

He found both through an open doorway to the right of the living room that led to the kitchen. It was tidier than the other room, and after washing his hands, he filled the kettle and set it to boil on the large gas stove. Searching the cabinets for tea and mugs, he heard Anais speaking in a soothing, gentle voice.

"Why don't we get you settled on the couch and you can tell me what you've been doing so far. I'm sure it's all good stuff, so I won't need to do much."

Their voices drifted into low murmurs, and he started making tea with honey. A coach had recommended it for him one fall season in high school when he'd been coughing more than catching balls. It was his go-to when he wasn't feeling great, even if it wasn't as effective as the horrible-tasting medications his parents would prescribe him. Later he'd learned there were more appetizing options available in the pharmacy, but he figured honey tea never hurt either. He brought a steaming mug out to the living room, then stopped in his tracks at the scene he stumbled into.

Anais was crouched low beside the couch, a stethoscope around her neck and a hand on her aunt's wrist. The old woman was wrapped in blankets, just her head and one arm out, and was listing off the various treatments she'd been doing. Her niece—Dr. Miller—was nodding, an encouraging smile on her face.

This was such a different kind of medicine than his parents practiced. They were all about perfection, the complicated procedures they performed proof of their superiority. They were the kind of people who looked at how much money you had, how much they could get out of you, how much a patient could do for them.

It was even different from the way the league doctors were with him. Jackson was there to do a job, and their job was to make sure he could do it. They weren't there to coddle him.

Anais was definitely a coddler. Maybe she'd been more tough-love with Bastien, but he'd test anyone's patience when he was sick or grumpy. Even when irritated with her brother, it was clear that Anais was the kind of doctor who gave everything she had to her patients. The kind of doctor who cared about patients as people, who saw the laugh lines and knew the stories behind each one. Hell, she'd probably been there for most of those stories.

The tender way she tucked the blanket around her aunt was something even his parents had never done for him. Maybe a nanny had, when he was really little. He knew he'd done it for his sister almost every night before he'd moved out.

A burst of emotion made its way up his chest and threatened to spill out of his eyes. He put the tea down on the coffee table, grabbed a few empty mugs, and rushed back into the kitchen before either of them noticed him. The mugs went into the sink, where he filled them up with soapy water. Then he placed his hands against the edge of the counter and leaned on them, breathing deeply through his nose. The same trick he used to get centered and focused before a game should have worked now too.

Except it was doing the opposite. Instead of facing down fastballs and first basemen, he was trying to ignore the very real feelings that were shifting inside of him. In baseball, he knew what he could do, what his body was capable of. His feelings for Anais were entirely new, and he had no idea what to do about them.

Of course, it was at that moment that Anais came into the kitchen.

"Are you okay?"

She put a hand to his wrist, checking his pulse, and her eyes were crinkled up with concern. With a heavy heart, he pulled his hand out of her reach.

"I'm fine. How's your Aunt Deb?"

"She'll be okay." Anais crossed her arms and leaned against the counter, facing him. "She's not dehydrated and her fever isn't too bad. I called in the prescription, and Clementine will drive it down later this evening. I'll check in on her tomorrow, since her phone is still out of service."

"I can drive you."

There was no reason for him to offer that. Her car would probably be fine by then. They hadn't set any rules around how things were supposed to be between them, but he was pretty sure she hadn't pictured their alone time being spent in a car on the way to see a sick relative.

Maybe she'll want to see me anyway.

"Thanks, I should be okay tomorrow."

Maybe not.

There was a pause, a beat, where something passed in the air between them. They were alone in the kitchen, facing each other. His hands were pressed into the counter just inches away from where her back was pressed into it. There was no noise other than their slow inhales and exhales. Her eyes met his, and the breath froze in his lungs at the look she gave him.

"You sure?" His voice was a low growl.

Her tongue darted out to lick her lips.

"Or you could drive me. I mean, if you have the time."

"I'll have the time."

"Great, so it's a date." Her cheeks tinged pink. "Not a date."

No, not a date. It couldn't be a date, but it still felt like a victory.

"What time should I pick you up?"

"I'll call you."

"You don't have my number."

Without a word, she held out her phone. Briefly, he considered putting his number under something cheeky, like "world's hottest first baseman" or "your brother's cute friend."

Instead, he did what he normally did and put his name as Jackson with a heart emoji after.

When he handed back the phone, she rolled her eyes.

"Really? A heart?"

He put on the sly grin that worked with so many women. "Just making sure I'm the only Jackson in your heart."

There was a sharp intake of breath and her hand shook again.

"I . . . " She swallowed hard. "I should go check on Aunt Deb one more time before we go."

Mother of pearl, what was he doing? She'd made it clear this was a temporary thing, purely physical, then his dang competitive streak had to go and take it way too far.

She's the one who asked for help.

No, she'd asked Bastien, who'd asked Jackson. That wasn't the same thing. Just because she wanted to spend a few weeks making out, just because she might not be a cold, heartless surgeon like his parents, didn't mean she saw him as someone worthwhile. And that was fine, really. It was better this way.

"Ready to go?" She appeared in the kitchen, bag slung over her shoulder, the earlier tightness in her eyes almost totally gone. The relief he felt to see her so much more relaxed sent a thousand alarm bells off in his head.

"Sure."

He followed her out, his head knowing things would end, but his stupid, hopeful heart still wishing there was another way.

THIRTEEN
ANAIS

Once again, Anais was dragging herself to Carl's Café due to complete exhaustion. Except the reason she was tired wasn't because of her brother, but because of his best friend.

"You okay, Anais?" Carl's kind eyes crinkled at the edges with concern.

She quickly slapped a smile on her face. Nobody wanted the doctor to look sick. That wouldn't be good for their confidence in her, especially with the flu going around.

"Fine. Just another late night."

A late night thinking about Jackson. Tossing and turning until three o'clock, dissecting every word he'd said to her the day before.

There hadn't been many words during the quiet drive back to town from Aunt Deb's, and they all seemed to have deeper meaning when she thought back on them. He probably assumed she wouldn't want to talk much if she was worried about her aunt. The visit had done a lot to calm her anxiety, however. The old woman was stubborn, and really would have made a great doctor if she'd gotten the chance. Taking care of the animals on her farm had been her passion before age and time had caught up to her. It was a relief to be going back to see her, even if the thought of another tension-filled, mostly silent car ride with Jackson made her pulse quicken and mind race.

It wasn't the fun they'd agreed to. He must be so disappointed with her. Needing his help wasn't what he expected from her. Like a test she'd only gotten a B on, she knew she could have done so much better.

Hence her disrupted sleep and consequential bleary-eyed presence at the café.

"I'll add an espresso shot," said Carl with a wink, his familiar warmth tugging at her heart. There wouldn't be anything like Carl's Café or the Parson family in Boston.

"You're a treasure."

The caffeine would help with the tired body, but not with the tumult in her mind. Jackson was coming to pick her up from the office in a few hours. He had so many other things to do while he was here to help Bastien, there was no reason for him to go out of his way to drive her again.

He might just be a nice guy, she reminded herself as she waved to people coming into the café. He was generous in a way Anais wasn't used to seeing in men other than her dad and brother. Though Bastien could be *too* focused on others, to the point of wearing himself out. Jackson was altruistic without it taking over his entire personality. That didn't mean he wanted to spend all his time driving her around without any chance for the fun they'd agreed to.

The memory of his lips on hers brought a heat to her face that she prayed no one in the café would notice.

"Here you go, doc." Carl held out her steaming thermos. "On the house."

She smiled her gratitude and stuffed a twenty into the tip jar as soon as his back was turned.

A few sips of the hot beverage had her brain thinking a little clearer. She inhaled the sharp, nutty aroma and breathed out a sigh as she looked around the café full of familiar faces.

This is just a novelty thing, she reasoned. Jackson was someone new and temporary. Of course she'd be more interested in him than the guys she'd known since they were letting glue dry on their hands and avoiding her because she hadn't gotten a "cootie shot."

Feeling calmer—and more awake—than when she'd walked in, she headed out to her car. Avery had dropped it off that morning with a brand new tire, and she slid into her seat. After a few more rejuvenating sips, the travel thermos went into its holder in the console.

The next steps were clear: she should call Jackson and tell him not to come. Driving her to check on her aunt wasn't part of the deal. Their time together would just be something physical, something that they'd both forget as soon as he flew back to Arizona in a few weeks. By the time she left for her fellowship, by the time she met someone perfect for her there, he'd be a distant memory.

When she pulled her phone out of her pocket, however, there was already a message waiting. Jackson with a little heart next to his name. An excited shiver went through her. He was confident, no doubt about it. He knew what he wanted and went after it. It was obscenely attractive, something Anais looked for in a partner, but it always seemed to bite her in the backside eventually. That confidence relied on making herself smaller and adapting her dreams to fit into his. With Jackson, she didn't have to worry about any of that.

Jackson: STILL ON FOR 1 THIS AFTERNOON?

Her thumbs hesitated over her phone. It was an easy out. All she had to say was that she had appointments, or that she would drive herself. They could always meet up that night for some fun.

Anais: ABSOLUTELY :-)

The second she hit send, her chest clenched. Only a few more hours until she saw him.

Shaking her head at her own irrationality, she started her car and made the short drive down Main Street to the office.

Doctors trusted their gut. For whatever reason, hers was telling her to spend a little more time with him, even if it wouldn't be doing what a very different body part was clamoring for.

The morning was busy, but not as hectic as the previous days. When there was a block of totally empty time and just two people in the waiting room—both fifteen minutes early to their appointments—her dad asked everyone to come into the break room for a quick chat.

Anais took in his downcast expression. "Is everything okay?"

Her dad's face smoothed out and he smiled. "Everything's fine. I just thought you'd like to share the news with everyone about the staffing changes that will happen in January."

The floor shifted under her feet. The NPs looked at her expectantly, while Clementine frowned a little.

"You mean the fellowship?"

Her dad chuckled. "Was there somewhere else you were planning on going next year?"

An image of sitting in a grandstand watching Jackson play flashed through her mind, her family at her side. She shook her head, not quite believing her dad had finally come around to see things her way.

"Austin's agreed to come work here?"

"Yes, I just called to offer him the job, and he said yes."

That sneak. She'd have to hound him later about holding out on the information.

The news seemed to perk up Clementine and Anais held back a sigh. She'd have to have a talk with him about staying away from her little sister, even if Minnie's shyness would do most of the work for her.

Plastering a smile on her face, Anais told the NPs all about her fellowship in Boston, how she'd be able to increase her experience and knowledge in women's health, while Austin would be bringing his experience in emergency medicine to their small medical practice. Her dad was smiling, but she could see the sadness in his eyes and in the set of his shoulders. It was clear that he didn't want her to go, but he was done trying to stop her from doing something that she wanted and would benefit the town so much.

The two NPs wished Anais luck and everyone started talking about how useful it would be for Jasper Creek to have someone close by to deal with the increase in accidents over the past few years. Though they all laughed when they realized Bastien probably accounted for at least half of those.

When she got into the car a few hours later, she was feeling buoyed and cheerful in a way she hadn't for weeks.

"You look much less worried than you did yesterday," Jackson said at once.

"I got some good news this morning." Anais leaned back in her seat as he made the turn out of the parking lot.

"That's great." A smile spread across his face, lighting up his eyes. "Anything you'd like to share?"

"I need to call Austin first." She hadn't had time yet, and it wouldn't feel entirely real until her friend had confirmed that he'd be moving into her office in a few months.

Jackson's expression went from sunny to dark in an instant, his knuckles white where he gripped the steering wheel. "Guess it must be something only doctors would understand."

"What?" Anais turned in her seat, confused, before realization hit. A teasing smile spread across her face. "Jackson, are you . . . jealous of Dr. Gibson?"

Two lines appeared between Jackson's eyebrows. "No."

Her heart squeezed, her older-sister lie detector on high alert. He was definitely jealous.

"You shouldn't be. There's nothing going on with him."

"Not my business if there is."

"He's just a friend, a good friend, coming here to fill in for me so I can do a fellowship starting in January."

There was a pause while Jackson turned down another road. She hadn't had to give him directions at all. He'd already memorized the route.

"Really?" The question was quiet, almost as if he didn't trust her to answer honestly.

"Yes. He has his own reasons for leaving the hospital, that I'll worm out of him one way or another. It's not like he'd drop everything to come work in Jasper Creek just because I asked him to."

Jackson's eyes flicked to hers. "You'd be worth it."

The breath left Anais's lungs in a whoosh, her lie detector silent. He'd meant it. A flutter of painful hope caught hold in her chest.

"Austin's a nice guy, but he's not that nice."

Jackson snorted. "What doctor is?"

"Excuse me?" Her voice was an octave higher than a moment before as emotional whiplash rocked her. Who went from saying something so sweet to something so rude?

"Aw, hell, I forgot who I was talking to."

Shaking his head, Jackson slowed the car to a stop on the side of the road. Heart pounding, Anais looked around. They weren't far from the farm on this empty stretch of a narrow road. Jackson looked like he was fighting a losing battle with himself to run straight out of the car and into the thick woods that surrounded them.

Avoiding her fuming gaze, he ran a hand across the back of his neck. "Did Bastien ever tell you that my parents are doctors?"

The hot anger racing through her veins cooled a few degrees. "No, he didn't."

"They're surgeons, in Charleston."

She inhaled slowly, the rest of her outrage melting away. Things he'd said before started to click into place. "They didn't want you to play baseball, did they?"

"They wanted me to be a doctor, like them. Make more money for the family, keep the Hart name connected to all the important, rich people in town."

Anais tried to imagine having parents like that, but it was impossible for her. Though she did understand what it was like to have her own goals feel not as important as what someone else wanted for her life. "That sounds like a really hard way to grow up."

"It was." His eyes finally met hers, and they were full of an old pain, before hardening off, like he'd clearly had to do his whole life. "They were big on looking perfect. Being out on the baseball field was the only place I could . . . I dunno, get dirty and have it be okay, you know?" He ran a hand through his hair.

She nodded, her fingers playing at the edge of her own hairline. "It's not easy to feel like everyone is watching you and judging you all the time."

There were few places she could be herself and not have the eyes of the whole town on her. Though it was different for her, with parents and a family she was proud of. She didn't mind that pressure. She was proud to be a Miller, and was determined to make sure she lived up to all those expectations.

"I figured you'd understand." He rubbed the back of his neck again. "Anyway, sorry I said that about doctors."

"It's fine." And it was. Knowledge was reassuring for Anais, and more of it made Jackson less mysterious. And—though she hadn't thought it possible—even more attractive. "I'm sure I've said some mean things about athletes too."

The corner of his lips tugged up. "Because of Bastien?"

"You only knew him in college. He was insufferable in high school."

Jackson laughed, and he checked the rearview mirror before signaling his entry back onto the road.

They were just about to turn into the farm when he spoke again. "What's the fellowship?" His tone was light, conversational, but the two lines had appeared between his eyes again.

"It's in women's health, in Boston."

"That's far." His eyes darted to hers again. "From your family, I mean."

Boston was also far from Washington state, where he played. She inhaled slowly, trying not to read too much into his comments, into how much he'd just shared with her. It didn't make something other than their short-term arrangement any more of a possibility for them.

"I'm used to it."

"But you'd never live that far from them permanently."

It wasn't a question, it was a statement. A sad one.

"No, I don't think I ever could."

The car filled with silence again as he parked in front of Aunt Deb's house. The realization seemed to sink in for them both. Whatever was between them, there was no way to make it work long-term. Her life was in Jasper Creek, even if it would be temporarily in Boston. His life would always be somewhere else.

Might as well enjoy him while he's here.

Turning to him, she leaned across the seat and touched her lips to his briefly, a promise of more to come once the work was done. The kiss deepened when his strong hand gripped the back of her neck and held her close.

The simmering tension that flickered between them whenever they were together turned up to eleven. Every nerve ending in her body lit up. She felt the kiss from the top of her head right down to her toes. It was like flying with her feet still on the ground. It was like a giant bowl of Moose Tracks. No, it was *better* than a giant bowl of Moose Tracks.

Way before she was ready for it to end, he pulled away, a smile dancing on his mouth and his blue-brown eyes alight with the same fire whooshing through her veins.

"I'll wait in the car."

"Good idea." If her aunt was feeling better, she'd notice immediately what was going on between Anais and Jackson. The last thing they needed was for her family to get wind of this. They'd make more of it than it was.

And it's nothing, she told herself as she hopped out of the car. The urge to look back was strong, but she kept her eyes on the front door, her years of training letting her focus her attention exactly where it needed to be.

He'd be there when she was done checking on Aunt Deb, and he'd be there for another week. Plenty of time to enjoy his kisses and get him fully out of her system.

When her head turned, against every conscious direction she'd given it, his eyes were fixed on her, his gaze intense. Blood rushed to her face, and she looked away quickly, inhaling deeply before she knocked on the door.

A plan was starting to take shape in her mind. After all, she should be prepared in case this thing between them turned out to be more than just something fun.

It had been a long time since Jackson had felt so good. Even with his aching wrist a constant reminder that he still hadn't heard back from the hospital, despite calling every day for updates, he found his spirits were high as he drove out to the high school on Friday afternoon. He parked, then strode over to the bench where Bastien was sitting. He wasn't alone.

"You remember my brother, Elias, right?" Bastien gestured to the lanky teen sitting next to him, who had a bat slung over his shoulder and a mitt in his hand.

"Of course." Jackson held out a hand and was surprised at the firm shake he got in return. "You almost beat Bastien at last week's game night."

Elias's eyes lit up. "You should have been there last night. I annihilated him."

When Bastien grunted and crossed his arms, Jackson laughed. "Now I'm really sorry I missed it."

He'd agreed with Anais, in between breathless kisses when he'd dropped her off the day before, that it would have been impossible to hide what was going on between them if he went to family game night. Even now, he could still feel the press of her body, the heat of her mouth.

So he'd told Bastien he was worried he was getting sick, and Clementine had come to pick him up instead. Jackson spent the night alone, wishing he could have at least sat across from Anais, even if his eyes would have revealed to all the Millers exactly what he wished he could be doing with her instead.

"Bash asked you about helping me with my swing, right?"

"That's why I'm here."

It wasn't what Jackson had thought he'd be doing when he'd agreed to stay another few weeks in Jasper Creek, but if it was what would help Bastien the most, then that's what he'd do.

As they walked down, Bash hopping along on his crutch, Jackson breathed in the cool autumn air. It was nice to be out on a ball field, even if it was a high school.

Maybe especially because it was a high school, actually. His own memories of his time spent playing, the pride that he'd felt over every point he won for his team, knowing it was getting him that much closer to his goal and that much further away from the life his parents had laid out for him.

Watching Bastien instruct his younger brother as he stepped out onto the plate put an entirely different feeling in Jackson's chest. It was an ache for something he'd never had. The more time he spent in Jasper Creek, the more he saw just how unusual his upbringing had been. The only place he'd felt even a fraction of the kind of acceptance he saw between the Millers was with the other players on his team.

Even that had a temporary quality to it, however. They were teammates until they got traded. Until someone got their shot at a spot on the regular roster. They were all happy for the other guys, but some of them passed in and out of the lower levels so quickly, you barely got time to know their names.

Jackson thought he'd be one of those guys, but that's not how his luck had played out.

He had to keep believing this was the year things were finally changing, even with his fractured hand and delayed surgery. The only other option was to consider a life without baseball. It would mean a life without achieving any of his dreams, without helping Madison get the life she wanted. He wasn't ready to think about what that looked like yet.

"Tighten up your grip a bit," Jackson yelled from his seat in the bleachers. "Widen your stance."

It was a sign of just how small the town was that Bastien was both the soccer and baseball coach. Bash knew soccer, of course, but learning the intricacies of another sport took time, and a passion that his friend had never shared for America's Favorite Pastime. Bash knew enough to get his team scoring runs, but not enough to make the kids great.

Elias was already a senior, and all set to go to Centennial University the following year, so he wasn't relying on baseball to get him through college. But it was clear the kid loved the game. Just because his brother wasn't the best coach didn't mean he shouldn't be able to play the best he could.

Jackson cupped his hands around his mouth. "That's better!"

"Why don't you come down here and show him instead of yelling like some cranky old man?" Bastien wobbled on his crutch when he turned around to holler up at Jackson. He could only use one, since his shoulder was hurt, and it made him a little unsteady.

In a flash, Jackson sprinted down the bleachers to stand next to Bastien, to offer his arm. By the time he got there, he was already stable, helped by Elias, who was glancing around nervously.

"If Anais saw you standing around like this, she'd have a fit."

The fear of invoking the wrath of his older sister was almost comically visible on the teenager's face.

"Is she really that scary?" Jackson chuckled. "She didn't seem that bad the other night when she was patching up Bastien for the second time in a week."

Bash waved a hand as Elias led him over to the dugout. "She isn't. El's just traumatized from the time he scraped his knee, and Anais wrapped him up like a mummy."

"She told me if I took it off, my leg would fall off." Elias flushed. "I was only six, so I believed her."

"I did something like that to my sister when she was around the same age." Jackson smiled at the memory. Protecting Madison had always felt like a full-time job when he was still at home. She'd been such a rambunctious kid. "She fell out of a tree in our yard when I was watching her, and I told her it made the tree mad and it would grow into her room if she didn't stay away from it forever."

"Older siblings can be a little evil, can't they?"

"Evil?" Bastien looked offended from his seat in the dugout. "We're not the ones falling out of trees and scraping up our legs. We're just trying to watch out for you little terrors."

"Who're you calling little?" Already over six feet, Elias was a few inches taller than Bastien. He'd probably grow another few inches before he stopped. He had that same tall, weedy look Jackson had at his age. Bastien was more muscled, with a broader chest.

Jackson's head was spinning at the similarities between him and Elias. Would he have chosen medicine like Elias had if his parents had been more like the Millers? The kid clearly loved the sport, but was willing to give that up to do what his family expected. Of course, you needed more than love to make it as a player, but it did help you get through the hard times a lot easier.

Jackson inhaled and shook his head, clearing away the cobwebs. "Okay, let's see that swing again."

After a few more adjustments, Jackson was satisfied that Elias understood what was needed. A group of guys was heading toward the field and one of them called out to Elias.

"We should go." Jackson turned to Bastien sitting on the sidelines, but Bash gestured for him to stay.

"Elias may have mentioned to a few of his friends that he was getting some time with a pro ballplayer."

Jackson frowned. He wasn't anybody special. He was still in the minor leagues, making peanuts, possibly at the tail-end of a career where he'd never get called up to The Show. "Are kids that easy to impress these days?"

"What are you talking about?" Elias stared at him. "You're great. You know way more than Bastien."

"That's not hard to do. I at least know which way to hold the bat."

"Hey! I heard that."

The swirling, nervous energy wouldn't leave Jackson's gut, however. When the other kids arrived and took out their bats and gloves, they all looked at him like he knew the secret to happiness.

Thinking of secrets naturally brought to mind memories of kissing Anais, but he pushed them away. He was there with her brothers. This was not the right time to be having those thoughts.

Compared to the prospect of dealing with two pissed-off Miller men, one with a bat and one with a crutch, helping a group of teen boys practice batting suddenly seemed like the easiest thing in the world.

"Step up to the plate. Let's see what we're working with."

All his troubled thoughts faded away with the steady sound of swinging bats and the comforting rhythm of an afternoon on the ballfield. If he just could do this forever, everything would be all right.

The next day was a long one, full of Halloween festival preparations.

"How well do you know this Austin guy?" Jackson asked Bastien while they were working on the lights for the storefronts on Main Street.

"Austin? You mean Dr. Austin Gibson?"

Bastien looked up from the bottom of the ladder, where he was holding it steady while Jackson hung orange lights around the edge of the door. Why the store owners weren't doing this, Jackson wasn't sure, but he suspected it was because in previous years Bastien had done it for them. A sprained ankle and shoulder weren't going to stop him from going overboard, not now that Jackson had agreed to stay and help.

"Yeah, him. He was at the office the other day talking to your sister."

"He's a friend of Anais's from her residency."

"She told me that already." Just because she said they were only friends didn't mean they'd always stay that way. "Do you all know him?"

"Some." Bastien passed up another string of lights. "He works at CUH, so he knows my mom. He's been out here a few times for parties and stuff. He'll probably be at the festival if he's not on call."

The muscles in Jackson's shoulders tightened. A family friend, but not a best friend to anyone, so totally not off-limits the way Jackson was. And he was a doctor.

"Why do you ask?" There was no suspicion in his voice, but lots of curiosity.

Jackson took a moment to adjust the lights before he answered.

"They just seemed really close, that's all."

"Well, he is one of her best friends. And he's taking over her role at Miller Family Medical while she's away on her fellowship."

"She told me that too. Why's she going all the way to Boston?"

"You're really that interested in the intricacies of medical fellowships?" From below him, Bastien raised an eyebrow.

"No, of course not. Just making conversation." Jackson busied himself with the lights for a few minutes, adjusting them exactly how Bastien told him. It required concentration, not just to handle the lights but to resist the urge to climb down the ladder and punch Bastien for being so picky. Either way, Jackson was grateful for the distraction from his stormy emotions.

Phil still didn't have an update from the team. Being put on waivers was looking more and more likely, but no other team would want him if he was injured. With his surgery date still up in the air, the possibility of him playing in the spring was less and less certain. Though Phil had offered to call the hospital for Jackson, that was an even less appealing option than asking one of Bastien's parents for help.

Maybe I could talk to Anais about it. She hadn't recoiled from what he'd told her about his family, and didn't seem to look at him as less valuable because he'd been vulnerable. She was a doctor who really cared.

All he could think about was when he'd get to kiss her again, to feel the kind of release he usually could only find on the ball field. There'd even been a few moments when he'd wondered what a future might look like with her. It gave him that same kind of shiver of excitement and achievement he got from that perfect crack of the bat on a pitch no one thought he could hit. Nothing and no one had filled his mind this way until he'd met Anais.

Except what kind of future could he offer her? All the money he saved was for Madison, and it wasn't much. Driving Anais around to home visits and helping Bastien with town festivals wasn't going to make him rich, and it wasn't exactly the high-profile career someone like Anais would be looking for.

No, asking her for help with his surgery was totally out of the question. So was telling her just how at risk his career was.

Lights done, he descended the ladder to face Bastien.

"What's next?"

Bastien raised his eyebrows. "Really? You still want to do more? We've been at this all afternoon."

It was true. The lights were the tenth thing they'd checked off Bastien's eighteen pages of to-dos for the Halloween festival set up. They'd been up since six that morning, even though it was a weekend. Bash had given Jackson a list of things to buy, then they'd spent over four hours doing various tasks around Jasper Creek.

Lights on the storefronts, check.

Lights on the gazebo in the park, check.

Booth tables moved from storage in town hall to the park, check.

Broken tables fixed, check.

Throughout every task, Bastien had been the one giving directions. It would be a lie to say that Jackson hadn't snapped a few times, but overall, the day had gone well.

Faced with a long evening of playing video games with Bash while pretending he wasn't thinking about Anais, Jackson didn't want to stop working just yet.

"I could do with the distraction," he told Bastien honestly.

His friend nodded slowly. "Still no word from Phil, huh?"

"*Yes*," he said, a little too enthusiastically. That made much more sense than mooning over Bash's sister. And less likely to get him a kick in the groin. "The World Series ended yesterday. They'll be reaching out to free agents in a few days, then they'll probably get around to deciding what to do about me."

"You sure you don't want to go see my mom about getting a new surgery date? She knows everyone at CUH."

Jackson rubbed the back of his neck. "I'll be fine."

"Okay, just let me know. I'm sure she'd be happy to help." Bash winced when he shifted his weight. "I think I'm done for the day though."

"Of course." Jackson grabbed the ladder. "What's the plan for tonight?"

They started the slow walk back to the car. Bash's ankle was getting better, but it was his first day without crutches, and he was still a little unsteady. It would have been faster for Jackson to go get the car, but he knew how important it was to feel capable again after an injury.

"Floodline?" Bash's eyes lit up with hope but dimmed when Jackson shook his head, the same way he had all week. "You didn't like it last week?"

"I'm just not in the mood to see a bunch of people." Or in the mood to pass by Anais's house without a valid reason to knock on her door. "If we show up again at your sister's door at two in the morning with you moaning in pain, she might actually kill me."

Bastien waved that away with the hand that wasn't wrapped in a bandage. "Oh, she'll get over it. What if I promise to be really, really good?"

Jackson laughed. "Well, I don't want to keep you from having fun. I can drop you off though, if someone can give you a ride back?"

They'd reached his car. "Of course. I'll ask Minnie if she wants to go."

Was there really no one else in town he could rely on? His friend seemed to do everything for everyone. They were all happy to laugh at his antics and take advantage of his generosity, but apparently no one could give him a ride home from the bar.

Sticky guilt coated his throat, and Jackson's need for a break battled with his promise to help his friend while he was here. Living alone in the off-season was a welcome relief after months on the road with twenty guys all shoved into a tiny bus. He loved his teammates, loved Bastien, but sometimes a guy just needed his space.

They got into the car and set off toward Bastien's house.

"Should I drop you off now?"

"I should change first." Bastien looked down at his clothes and gave a quick sniff. "What'll you eat? There's nothing in my fridge. You could pick up something at the Floodline."

"I'll figure something out." Jackson's lips turned up. "I can't eat burgers every night and stay in shape like we could in college."

The second he said it, an idea popped into Jackson's head. Being the more responsible twin, Anais was sure to have healthy food in her kitchen. He wasn't in the mood for the crowds of the Floodline, but he was definitely in the mood for some one-on-one time with her.

"Okay, well, thanks for all your help today." Bastien put a hand on his shoulder. "Really. I don't know what I would have done to get everything ready without you."

Finally told someone in town to step up and help you, hopefully.

"Of course, man. Happy to help."

FIFTEEN
ANAIS

It had really been too much to expect that no sleep and dealing with flu patients for three days straight would mean Anais could escape getting sick herself. Even though she'd gotten her flu shot at CUH as soon as they were available, and even though she'd been wearing a mask in the office with patients. Despite their best efforts, even doctors got sick sometimes, and Anais had been more stressed and tired than she'd been since her first year of residency.

That late night this weekend with Jackson probably hadn't helped either.

She shivered underneath the three layers of blankets she was buried under on the couch, and not from the cold.

When he texted her Saturday night to ask if she had any food in her fridge, she hadn't expected him to show up with a pint of ice cream from the Floodline, and no Bastien in sight.

Their evening together had been fantastic, and it wasn't just her fever-addled brain thinking that. Though through her haze of illness, the plan to keep him firmly in the "temporary fun" category was starting to seem like a fantastically bad idea.

She snuggled deeper into the blankets and groaned, the

sound muffled. This wasn't the time to worry about that. This was the time to focus on getting better.

So I can kiss him again.

No.

Her eyes flew open and she sighed. What she needed—other than another dose of Guaifenesin for her stuffy nose and a refill of her water glass—was a distraction. Monday at the office, it had been easy to focus on her patients and forget about Jackson.

Today her only patient was herself, and she was a grumpy one. This called for bad daytime television, the kind she never got to watch because she was working.

She fell asleep halfway through a soap opera with characters she didn't recognize but suddenly cared deeply about. Her dozing brain finished up the story, replacing the male lead on the show with Jackson.

The dream, as so many of her best ones lately, was interrupted by the doorbell ringing.

With another groan, Anais threw the blankets off and dragged herself to the door.

"Bash, I swear if you hurt yourself again, I'm going to cough all over you."

The effort it took to open the door turned what was supposed to be an irritated fling into more of a slow creak. Hopefully it looked dangerous, not weak, and he wouldn't notice her hands trembling with cold.

"No injuries, but I think I'll leave the soup out here just to be safe."

Her already shivering body froze. It wasn't her brother, it was Jackson.

The fuzzy memory of the soap-opera-inspired dream still lingering in Anais's mind, she stood there with her mouth hanging slightly open.

Though to be fair, she could only breath with her mouth open at the moment.

"Uh, you look like you might drop this." Jackson held up a to-go bag from Carl's Café. "Can I come in? Or is the coughing all over me still on the table?"

Anais shook her head and cleared her throat. "I'm sorry, sure, come in." She stepped back to let him in. "I thought you were Bastien."

"Did you tell him you were sick?" Jackson asked as he made his way down the hallway to the kitchen. It was weird but nice to have him there, to see how he already knew his way around. Anais followed in a slow shuffle.

"No, but I told my dad, so everyone in the family knows." She paused at the entrance to her kitchen, watching Jackson open cabinets. His tremendous trapezius muscles flexed under his thin gray t-shirt when he reached up and pulled out a bowl. "How did you hear, if not from Bastien?"

"I was getting coffee at the café, and I think there must be a few people out sick. Carl looked pretty overwhelmed." Jackson opened the paper bag and lifted out a cylindrical container filled to the brim with what looked like chicken noodle soup. "I saw this on the counter with your name on it and told him I could deliver it if he needed help."

The generosity of Jackson shouldn't have stunned her at this point, but her heart gave a squeeze anyway. She propped herself up more steadily on the doorframe as she watched him pour the soup into the bowl. By the time he turned around with the bowl in his hands, she'd managed to school her expression into something slightly less gawking.

He frowned at her. "Get back to the couch. I'll bring this out."

"You don't have to take care of me."

"I want to take care of you."

Her knees wobbled at the sincerity of his words. *He doesn't mean it like that.* The temporary fun they'd agreed to didn't make him her boyfriend, didn't make this caretaking anything more than Jackson being the kind, generous man he was.

He lifted his chin, nudging her away from the doorway and back into the hallway. She shuffled slowly back to the couch and settled in again under her piles of blankets while he laid the bowl on the coffee table.

"Clementine probably ordered it for me." It was just soup, but Anais ached at the reminder of how hard it would be to have her family far away when she was inevitably sick during her year in Boston. Shifting so that the blankets were wrapped around her shoulders, she lifted the bowl to her nose. She inhaled, but she was still too stuffy to get more than the barest whiff of chicken. "She's really thoughtful like that. She'll make a good doctor."

"Hmm." Jackson settled into the chair across from her.

"What?" Anais took a sip and closed her eyes, letting the warmth spread down into her chest. When she opened them again, Jackson was frowning again. "You don't think Clementine will be a good doctor?"

"I reckon she'll be amazing like you." He shifted in the chair with a thoughtful look on his face. "But are you sure that's what she wants to be?"

Anais set down the soup on the table, harder than she intended and it splashed onto her hand.

Jackson was up in a flash. "I'll grab a napkin."

In the time it took him to get one, Anais considered his words. Had Clementine said something to Jackson? Even if they'd only met a few times, Anais could understand why her sister might open up to him. Considerate and courteous, he'd make an amazing husband one day—for someone other than Anais.

The second he was back in the room, she pounced. "Why wouldn't she want to be a doctor?"

Jackson sighed and wiped off the table.

"I don't know. Is there a reason she should be a doctor?"

"Millers have been doctors in Jasper Creek for almost a hundred and fifty years. Practically as long as there's been a town here."

"And you've got two of them now. Isn't that enough?"

"My dad is slowing down. He can't go on for decades." He'd been doing it all on his own since his brother had passed away unexpectedly when Anais was in college. It was why she'd pushed herself to finish undergrad a year early so she could help him sooner. "It made sense for Bastien not to go into medicine. He was all about sports since he was a toddler. But Clementine was pre-med. She's applying to med schools. A doctor is what she wants to be."

"Did she say that or is it just assumed that's what she'll be?"

Anais rubbed her hand against her forehead. This wasn't what she thought they'd be talking about, and she was in no shape for a fight.

As perceptive as ever, Jackson reached out and touched her arm. "Hey, I'm sorry. I didn't mean to upset you." He withdrew his hand and Anais felt the lack of it like an ache. He sighed and sat down again, his face tight with exhaustion.

"I'm surprised you're not sick, too, considering . . . Well, you know." Hopefully the heat in her face looked like the flush of a fever, and not because she was thinking about all they'd done together over the past week.

"I've never gotten sick."

"Never?" She tried to give him her best *I know you're lying* glare, but it was probably less effective with a blanket draped over her shoulders like a cape.

He rubbed the back of his neck. "My parents didn't like to see me sick."

"No parent does."

"No, I mean, they saw it as a sign of weakness or something. Like I was bothering them, like it was shameful for the son of doctors to get sick. It made them look bad, like they weren't good doctors."

"That's completely ridiculous. Everyone gets sick."

When the words left her mouth, though, she knew she didn't fully believe them. Hadn't she fretted over people in town seeing her look tired, or with shaking hands? She abhorred the thought of anyone thinking she was vulnerable, worried that they wouldn't trust her as a doctor.

The soup churned in her stomach. Was she just as bad as his parents?

Jackson ran a hand over his hair and looked out the window. "Anyway, it was good practice for playing ball. You play even when you're sick."

"You shouldn't push through like that. It can't be good for the team to have people playing sick."

Jackson gave a humorless laugh. "This isn't a regular job. We don't get sick days. We're paid next to nothing. We don't play, we don't get seen, we don't get a shot at moving up."

The hours of minor league research she'd done had told her as much. It was frankly disgusting how little they were paid, when major league players made millions. "Is it really worth it?"

"I wouldn't still be playing if it wasn't." He looked back at her and a funny smile spread across his face. "I think I love it even more because it's hard, you know? If everyone could do it, then it wouldn't be as special. Kind of like being a doctor."

She snorted. "I'm not some genius just because I can name all the bones in the body. A good doctor is about caring. Everyone can do that."

"Not everyone does, though."

The more he shared, the more it broke her heart to think of this gorgeous, sweet man put down by the same people who were supposed to be lifting him up. That's not what family was supposed to be, and that's all Jackson knew. It's what he expected from her, from everybody. There had to be some redeeming quality he just wasn't seeing in his family.

Abandoning her soup, Anais leaned back on the couch and propped her head in her hands to look at him. "Did your parents really not care at all?"

"They wanted me to be a doctor. Like them." His lips thinned out. "They didn't really care if I was happy or not about it. It's what the Harts in Charleston do."

"Is living up to a legacy really that terrible a thing? It's what I'm doing."

"Except you have a legacy you can be proud of." Jackson dropped his arms to his knees and shook his head. "The Millers do it because they care about the people in this town. My parents just care about money and prestige."

She blinked at that. "A professional baseball player doesn't have money or prestige?"

"Not when you've been stuck in the minors your entire career." He threw up his hands. "Some guys are happy with that. They just want to play ball for as long as they can."

"But not you?"

He looked at her, and the burning desire in his eyes told her what she needed to know. He wanted more. He wanted it all. He wanted to be the best he could be. She'd already suspected that a small-town life was the furthest thing from what he wanted, and here was the proof.

"I want to create my own legacy, on my own terms."

His fire, his passion, was deeply attractive. It reminded

Anais of how her dad talked about meeting her mom for the first time. How determined she'd been, how focused.

Except she'd been focused on medicine, just like him, so it worked out between them.

"Is there any news about next season?" The roughness of her voice would be attributed to her cough, and not the hope she was selfishly clinging to.

His eyes turned away, and his shoulders tensed. "Not yet."

She tucked her arm back underneath her and laid her head on the pillow.

"Thank you for bringing me the soup."

"You're welcome." He stood, brushing his hands on his pants. "I'll let you rest."

"No wait." She held out a hand, and he paused halfway out of his chair. "Can you stay, just a little while? Or do you have to go train or help Bastien or something?"

His eyes lingered on hers, a different kind of fire burning in them. "I'll stay as long as you want."

Satisfied, she smiled, snuggled back into the couch, and closed her eyes. Her brother and the Halloween festival preparations could wait another hour.

As disheartening as his answers had been, she hadn't totally given up on her new plan. There was baseball in Boston, after all. Maybe she could still have love in the same place her parents had, but bring it with her instead of finding it there.

She'd leave the details for tomorrow, when her head was clearer. For the moment, she'd take the soothing comfort his presence gave her, not questioning or worrying about what kind of heartache it might bring later if her plan didn't work out. If it didn't, she could always come up with a new one.

The air was bright and the sun was warm on Jackson's back as he ran along the river.

He'd gone three miles longer than he'd planned, but the distance was flying by. He felt lighter than air, like he could run a marathon and then play a double header.

It was ridiculous that a bit of—fine, a lot of—making out could have such an effect on him. But he knew it wasn't the stolen moments, it was the woman. Everything about Anais had been unexpected from the second he'd met her, and her kisses were no different. The mere memory of them gave him the energy of a guy ten years younger and no chronic injuries.

On cue, his knee gave a twinge. It wasn't a real injury, not like his hand, just something that had started happening more often the past year. He slowed his pace, but the muscles still protested.

He'd shared so much of himself with Anais, but he still held back all of the aches and pains. He hadn't told her yet how grim his last call with Phil had been. Even if he was put on waivers, even if he never played again, he couldn't stay in Jasper Creek. What would he even do here? They could never be permanent parts of each other's lives . . . except he'd always be friends with Bastien, so Anais would always be in his life in some way.

Unless Bastien beat him to a pulp and never spoke to him again once he found out about all the fun Jackson was having with his sister.

He slowed to a walk, sweat dripping down his face. He lifted the edge of his shirt to wipe it out of his eyes. The urge to call his own sister came over him, but it was the middle of the day and she was in class. Was he seriously considering asking his little sister for advice on girls?

His stomach turned. She might want to ask his advice about boys, and he much preferred not thinking about her dating until she was well into her forties.

A biker whirled toward him on the trail and he stepped aside to leave them space.

The irony of him hating the idea of his sister dating while also reminiscing about kissing his best friend's sister was not lost on him. As if to agree with his stupidity, his knee twinged again. He balled his hands into fists, which only made his wrist sing with pain.

"I know, I know," he said out loud.

He hadn't heard back from any of the surgeons yet. It had been weeks since he'd injured himself and things weren't going to get better magically. Centennial University Hospital was the number one hospital in the country for orthopedic surgery, and he wasn't going to risk his career on anything less than the best. This tiny piece of snobbery was the only part of his parents' legacy he had held on to over the years.

The most practical thing would be to ask Dr. Miller to call them, to see if she got a faster reply, but Jackson hated that he needed more help. Even from someone as nice as Anais and Bastien's mom. Maybe he could ask Clementine to call.

Clementine was a little older than his sister, Madison, but

the similarities were there. Both shy, both unsure about what path they wanted to follow. It had been years since he'd actually seen Madison, and they'd kept in touch with monthly phone calls. The split from his parents had happened when she was only eleven, and the first time he'd called her afterward, she'd barely wanted to speak with him.

He hadn't given up, though. Every month he'd called, on the first Sunday, like clockwork. She had her own phone by then, so it was easy to call without their parents knowing. Once she realized he was serious about staying in her life, despite the rift with their parents, she'd opened up. Those calls became his lifeline during the grind of the season and the loneliness and boredom of the off-season. She followed his career online, and asked him about his training every time they spoke.

There was a bench next to the river, and Jackson leaned against it, stretching out his quads. He didn't miss much about Charleston other than his sister, but he did miss the water. Running along the river was soothing and familiar.

Madison was in her second year of college, and sometimes when he called on Sundays she wouldn't answer, texting back that she was in the library. A part of his brain suspected that wasn't true, reminding him that she wasn't a little girl anymore. The big brother part of his brain reassured him that no, if she said she was studying, then she was.

The urge to hear her voice, to know that she was okay, was as overpowering as the endless flow of the river along the rocks lining its shore. Even though it was the middle of the week, he took a seat on the bench and tapped her name in his phone. She picked up immediately.

"Jackson, what's wrong?"

"Hello to you too, sis."

"Don't 'hello' me. It's not the first Sunday." There was a

tremor of panic in her voice. "Something must be wrong. Are you hurt?"

Rather than the timid Clementine, Madison sounded more like Anais and her analytical, observant ways. Anais's sharp, precise movements and careful but bold authority put Jackson at ease for reasons he didn't want to explore too deeply right now.

"Nothing's wrong. I'm just on vacation and had some time. I was thinking about you so I thought I'd call."

"Oh." She sounded surprised, but not relieved. "You're on vacation? Has that ever happened before?"

He chuckled and switched the phone to his other hand so he could stretch his other side. "I know, right? But I saved up last year so I have more breathing room. I don't need to deliver pizzas or drive a rideshare this winter."

"So, where are you vacationing? Somewhere warm, I hope?"

She'd heard him complain more than once about the winters in Washington, and she had the kind of brain that remembered every single detail.

"Colorado. I'm visiting a friend from college, Bastien."

"The one with a big family of doctors?"

Wow, she really did remember everything he'd ever said.

"That's the one."

"But he's not a doctor. I can see why you'd be friends." There was a rustling of papers and a soft voice in the background.

"Are you studying? I'm sorry I didn't mean to interrupt your morning."

"No it's fine, it's just this Orgo test I have coming up."

"I didn't know you're taking Organic Chemistry." Jackson's heart sank. "You decided on pre-med then?"

The year before, she'd been gabbing nonstop about all the

different classes she was taking, and how much she loved English and Art History. It had been such a positive sign that his example of breaking away from the pressure of generations of Hart doctors was giving her the confidence to carve her own path. He'd told Anais the low pay and playing while sick was worth it, and it was—so Madison could have whatever life she wanted.

But if she was pre-med, then the pressure from their parents must have been too much.

"Yeah, I declared my major. Biology." Her voice was small, hesitant, like it had been in those first calls all those years ago. Like she was afraid of saying something wrong and he'd get mad and never speak to her again.

He wasn't mad, but he couldn't just let her make that decision without realizing everything it implied. The conversation with Anais about Clementine was still on his mind. If someone with a big, loving family was terrified to step out of what was expected, how would Madison have any hope to do the same, with their parents the way they were?

"So med school is your goal? It's what you really want?"

"It's not like I play a sport or have some other talent to monetize. I have zero interest in doing anything influencer-y online like my friends from prep school." She sighed. "I know you want to help, but you're injured and out of options, and you're barely scraping by in the minors. I can't afford to do this on my own the way you did. It's different for women."

Jackson sat down heavily on the bench. That hurt most of all. The money he'd get if—no *when*—he made the majors wasn't just for him. It was to give his sister a way out, whenever she needed it.

And it sounded like she needed it sooner rather than later.

"Look, you don't have to decide anything now." He leaned his arms against his knees and ran a hand over his face. "Tell me about your other classes. Unless you have to get back to studying?"

"I could use a break."

She sounded happier as she talked about her Art History elective, the one non-science class she was taking that semester. Jackson walked along the river, the morning sun sparkling on the water, unable to keep the smile off his face as he heard her talk about all the paintings and sculptures she'd seen on a recent weekend in Charleston. Her private college was a few hours outside of the city, but she went home pretty regularly. Why, Jackson had no idea, since their parents were never home.

He could have kept talking to her for longer, but his phone buzzed with a text from Bastien asking if he wanted to get something to eat.

"Maddy, I've got to go."

"It was nice talking to you not on a Sunday."

He grinned. "You can call whenever you need to."

He said it every time he called, but she never took him up on the offer. It hadn't really bothered him, until he saw how Bastien was with his sisters. They were in constant contact, all living in the same town. It wasn't what Jackson had ever thought he wanted. But missing so much of her life and being so far from Madison for so long was starting to take a toll.

Once he'd made it to the majors, he'd be set. If she still wanted to study medicine, fine, he'd foot the bill. She could go to school in whatever town his team was in and he'd get her set up with someplace to live.

But what if he couldn't? What if this injury was the thing that kept him from giving her everything she deserved?

He picked up his pace to a jog, his knee feeling better after the walking and stretching, but his mind was a total mess. There was a clear solution to his problem: asking Bastien's mom for help to get another surgery date. It just left too horrible a taste in his mouth to even consider it.

It wasn't that he had to do everything on his own. He was part of a team, after all, and no single player could win a game. The coaches, the trainers, even the batboy were all essential to leading a team to victory.

It was in the rest of his life where using backend, sneaky deals made his skin crawl. It was too much like his parents' world, too much like how they operated. It was how they'd expected him to act as he got older. Even the thought of a player having to call Phil to get out of trouble with the police was unimaginable to Jackson. Avoiding breaking the law had more to do with Jackson never wanting to have to call anyone to bail him out than it did with actually respecting those laws.

The buildings on the outer limits of Jasper Creek came into view, and he caught sight of the high school baseball field where he'd coached Elias and his friends. A different kind of future prickled at the edges of his mind.

If he didn't get the surgery, maybe this thing with Anais didn't have to be temporary. Maybe there was something he could do in town, a way for him to stay. Or something he could do in Boston, where she'd be next year. All these feelings he had for her could lead to something more. Whatever was happening between them was too intense to limit to a few weeks of hooking up in secret.

There was no way he could go to family game night, even though he'd told her he'd be there. Bastien would know immediately something was going on the instant Jackson laid eyes on Anais. He could hide his feelings on the ballfield but wasn't a good enough actor to hide something like that.

Instead of family game night, he'd spend the evening thinking about what to do next. It didn't seem like there was any way for everyone to get what they wanted. Thinking about staying with Anais was exciting, and felt like the right choice, and it meant he wouldn't have to deal with the hospital anymore. However, without getting his hand fixed, his baseball career would be over. He'd have to figure out a job, a future, one that would be enough for her and Madison. That terrified him more than facing down a switch pitcher in a tied game at the bottom of the ninth.

On the other hand, if he sucked it up and finally asked Dr. Miller for help getting his surgery, he would—maybe, hopefully—be able to keep playing. Then he'd have the career and status that would secure Madison's future, and make him—maybe, hopefully—a viable option for Anais.

There were a hell of a lot of unknowns in both options. Kind of like baseball. Even with stats you could analyze, and previous games to watch, a pitcher could be having an amazing night that sent a curveball whipping through your plans. Or unexpected injuries could change the lineup halfway through the game and relief players were brought in.

He could use a relief player for this decision. Both options sounded like the right one for different reasons. He'd never had to make a choice like this before. There had always been a clear path forward, only one direction he could go.

Arriving at Bastien's doorstep, he wiped his brow and stepped inside to find his friend waiting for him with takeout and the TV turned on.

Maybe he could just play video games and hope things would work themselves out on their own. Sometimes when a game was this close, praying for a miracle was all you could do.

There weren't many big events in town, but Anais had always loved the Halloween festival the most. It lasted three days and was full of the kind of small-town charm that the Hallmark channel had been trying to recreate for years. Bobbing for apples, pumpkin carving stations, a costume competition, a 5k charity race . . . and that was just what the town organized. Well, what Bastien organized.

Then there was a traveling carnival that would arrive soon, taking over the elementary school's sports field with rides and games.

Walking through the partially set up booths while high school volunteers finished the last of the decorations in the late-afternoon light, Anais felt calmer than she had all day. Being there, in the familiar, comforting chaos she'd missed for years was the perfect distraction from the disappointment of Jackson not showing up to family game night.

They hadn't seen each other since he'd come over with soup, and she'd been looking forward to spending the evening with him and her family. Instead, Bastien had shown up with Clementine, and didn't even mention his friend. It was like

Jackson had just disappeared from Jasper Creek without even a goodbye.

She'd lost miserably at Monopoly, which she normally won. Luckily, Elias had taken the attention off Anais's moodiness by gloating nonstop about his win.

The smell of cinnamon wafted over to her on the cool autumn breeze, taking Anais's mind off the previous night. Carlie Parson was stationed at a table right in the middle of the park, boxes of donuts piled high in front of her and a line of hungry people keeping Anais from getting one for herself. She joined the line and smiled at those who waved to her.

Elias appeared at her side and gave her a shove. "Hey, these are for volunteers, loser."

"I'm here to help, you snarky teenager." She didn't actually need to be there, but it was the only place she could think Jackson might be. Texting him should have been the simplest solution, but she hadn't been able to think of a way to phrase it that didn't sound like she was a jealous girlfriend checking up on him.

Elias said something to her, but Anais missed it completely. From the corner of her eye, she spotted two figures approaching —one limping and the other tall, dark, and most definitely Jackson.

Elias waved so hard, he bumped Anais in the face.

"Ow."

"Oops, sorry." He gave her a sheepish smile. "Do you think he'll stand with us?"

"Who, Jackson?"

Elias rolled his eyes. "No, I just waved like an idiot for our brother. Of course Jackson. Have you seen him play?"

Anais shook her head. Despite the temptation of easily accessible information on him thanks to the internet, she hadn't done any snooping. It didn't seem fair, not when he couldn't do the same for her. Though all he had to do was ask anyone in town for her life story and they could give it to him. She could ask Bastien about his friend, but whatever Jackson wanted to tell her was all she needed to know.

Hopefully he'd tell her why he hadn't come to game night.

"He's great." Elias rattled off a few of Jackson's stats. "So fast, great instincts. I don't know why he's still in the minor leagues."

The two men were getting closer, slowed by Bastien's unsteady gait. She made a note to check on his ankle at some point that evening.

"Well, don't bring it up, okay?" Anais gave him her best *listen to your older sister* glare. "This is contract negotiation season, so if he hasn't heard anything, don't make him feel bad."

Elias blanched. "Do you think that's why he didn't come last night?"

Now that he said it out loud, that did make sense. Jackson must have gotten some bad news and hadn't felt like being around a bunch of people all night. It made more sense than a sudden disinterest in Anais, especially after bringing her soup and taking care of her in such a tender way.

Bastien finally reached them. "Save any donuts for us?" he asked.

Jackson was hanging back a bit, and when he met Anais's eyes, he jerked his head. "Anais, I forgot something in the car. Can I get your help?"

She didn't even hesitate. "Grab me a donut, little brother."

"Which one?" Elias and Bastien called after her.

"Both of you!" She tried not to run in her eagerness to catch up to Jackson. Being near him after not seeing him for a few days was intoxicating. The air shimmered between them, her pulse crackling with anticipation. They walked all the way back to Bastien's car, parked on the other side of the gazebo.

"Why did you park so far away?"

"We got here late. I offered to drop Bastien off closer, but he said he'd be fine."

Anais pursed her lips. It wasn't what she'd have wanted as his doctor, but as his sister who wanted to make out with his best friend, the privacy was nice.

She peered into the car. "What did you need help with?"

"Oh, nothing. I just wanted to do this."

He grabbed her hand and pulled her behind the car, out of view of anyone. Their lips met once, twice, and his hands curled into her hair, pulling her close.

She melted into him, her arms wrapping around him and her fingers grabbing tight to his t-shirt, as if he might fly away if she didn't hold him down. The heat of his kiss spread through her body, relaxing her muscles so much she wobbled on shaking legs.

With a concentrated effort, she pulled out of his embrace to catch her breath. "Well, happy to help anytime." She giggled.

His face remained serious, however. "I'm sorry I wasn't there yesterday."

"It's fine." She reached a hand up to her forehead, but Jackson's was already there, pushing her hair back behind her ears. Her knees trembled at his gentle, thoughtful touch.

"I didn't come to family game night last week, so I thought it would be weird if I did this week."

"Jackson, you don't have to explain, you're not my—" Boyfriend wasn't even close to what he was to her, but there wasn't a good word to describe what this was. Hot interim hookup? Stress-relief makeout buddy? "You don't owe me an explanation. I know that whatever this is, it's temporary."

"What if it wasn't?"

Her heart shot into her throat.

"What do you mean?"

"I mean, things still aren't settled for next season."

This was what she'd been hoping for. A sign that he might consider staying in a town like Jasper Creek. Her heart started to race, making it hard to focus on his face.

Just breathe.

"I still have a fellowship. In Boston."

"And Austin will be here."

She raised an eyebrow at the jealous way he said Austin's name. "Well, someone has to help my dad while I'm gone."

"Why are you even leaving if you're worried about your dad?"

She inhaled sharply.

"It's important I get the experience." It wasn't a complete lie. It just wasn't the full truth. It was the reason she gave her family, to her patients, to people in town when they asked. "Having someone specialized in women's health will help the town so much."

It was also the only way for her to find someone who could really love her. Not that she could tell him that. It didn't make sense, not really. She was rational enough to realize that. It didn't change the fact that every man in town within five years of her age was either in a relationship, or only ever called her to make a medical appointment.

Jackson shook his head. "You and your brother seem to do more for this town than the mayor."

"Well, the Millers have always helped the town. It's just what we do." She looked up to meet his eyes in the fading light. "It must be the same back in Charleston. There are some families that are just . . . woven into the town's DNA. The expectation is there, and we meet it."

His eyes turned dark with emotion, and Anais took a step back.

"Yes, it is the same there." He frowned. "The Harts are that kind of family."

"So you get it."

He sighed. "Unfortunately, I do."

"I have to do this fellowship."

He ran a hand through her hair, sending shivers down her spine. "Boston is so far away."

The flutter in her stomach was barely calmed by another deep breath. "You really don't have any idea what's happening next season?"

The frown was back. "No. Still a few more days."

"But you could end up anywhere in the country, right?"

He hesitated, then nodded.

"I could never live with so much uncertainty." The moment the words were out of her mouth, she winced. "I shouldn't have said that."

"Why not? No one's around to hear it." He gave her a smile. "Even Dr. Miller is allowed to have doubts, isn't she?"

"I thought you said you understand how these kinds of things work." She sighed and leaned against him, burying her face in his muscles. "Any sign of weakness from me—"

"Makes the whole town worried. I get it." He moved his hand from her hair to run it reassuringly along her back. She relaxed into the warmth of it, of him.

"Do you really?" She burrowed into his chest. "It's important what people think of me here. A life in Jasper Creek is all I've ever wanted. When's the last time you were home?"

He stiffened under her and she rushed to explain.

"You don't have to talk about Charleston." He'd already shared so much about his parents, and why baseball had been his escape. It was clear the topic was a tough one for him. "I just mean, baseball is kind of an itinerant life, isn't it?"

"I've been with the Wildcats since I was twenty."

"That's a long time with one team." A happy buzz filled her chest. Maybe he *was* the kind of man who wanted the same things as her. Someone who found something he believed in and stuck with it, long-term.

He sighed, and she could feel his chest slowly move up and down. He settled his chin on top of her head and wrapped his arms around her. "I have been there a long time. It's probably time for something new."

Hope bubbled inside her. Had all the work with Bastien the past few weeks made him picture a new life? He was probably just waiting until he heard for sure from his team before saying anything.

"We should get back." Her mind whirring with possibilities, she stepped out of the warm circle of his arms.

"Just one more." The kiss that landed on her lips was a sweet, brief one, but it filled her with hope that he might just be thinking the same thing she was.

EIGHTEEN
JACKSON

If the vibe at Miller Family Medical was the unfamiliar one of cozy comfort, the vibe at Centennial University Hospital was the same one Jackson got every time he went to see his parents as a kid: a deep, murky dread that started in his stomach and made its way down into his legs, making them shake uncontrollably.

Perfectly normal reaction when walking into a hospital.

It hadn't been as bad when he'd met with the surgeon before his original surgery date at a medical office down the street from the hospital. While it had been a sterile, white-walled kind of place, it reminded him enough of the countless physical therapy offices he'd been in that he'd been able to keep his reaction neutral.

There was nothing neutral about his reaction now. As he walked through the atrium, his breaths were coming out in short bursts, like he'd just sprinted to home plate. His lungs didn't want to fill up with enough air. Pretending it was a game, and he was facing a pitcher with a wicked curveball, he kept his eyes on his target. In this case, it was the elevators at the other side of the large open atrium. Letting everything else fade away, he focused on those metal doors, blocking out the sounds and smells of the hospital. Once he was inside and heading upstairs, he could pretend it was just another office building.

Of course, he was so laser focused, he didn't realize the doors were actually closing as soon as he stepped up to them. He clenched his hands, and pain zinged through his wrist. A curse escaped his lips, but he refused to turn around and look anywhere else. He pummeled the up button like it had just insulted him. He was being ridiculous, he knew it, but what other choice did he have? Start shaking and screaming in the middle of a hospital? Turn around and run out the doors?

"Jackson?"

At the sound of his name, he turned his head to the side. His stomach dropped. It was the very last person he wanted to see.

"Dr. Gibson." He gave the other man a tight nod, then returned his gaze to the elevator doors that were still stubbornly closed.

"Here to see Dr. Miller?"

He didn't look at Austin when he nodded again.

"I'm happy to show you the way. The hallways here can get a little confusing."

"That's very . . . " Jackson looked for the right word. "Kind of you."

It wasn't like he thought doctors couldn't be kind. If nothing else, his time with the Millers had proven they weren't all money-hungry monsters like his parents. But despite what Anais had said, Jackson still saw Austin as a rival, and always would. He'd assumed the other man saw him the same way, and would take any opportunity to make his life as difficult as possible.

"Of course." There was a note of surprise in Austin's voice, and Jackson finally turned his head to look at him.

Compared to the other day in Jasper Creek, when he'd been

smooth haired and smiling with Anais at his side, Austin looked more than a little scruffy. More like Jackson at the end of a long bus ride home from a week of away games than a polished and professional doctor. His dark hair was rumpled, and his blue eyes were rimmed in red. There was no sign of the bright, shiny smile he'd been flashing at Anais the other day, and his face was pinched into so tight of a frown it looked painful.

"Are you okay?" Jackson found himself asking.

"What?" Austin blinked, then shook his head with a chuckle. "Oh yeah, just had a rough night."

For the first time, Jackson wondered what would be in it for Austin to come to Jasper Creek, other than Anais.

"It's not easy working in a hospital," Jackson said. It wasn't a question. He knew firsthand the toll it took on people and what it did to their relationships.

"You can say that again." Austin gave another chuckle, but it was hollow and mirthless.

The elevator finally dinged, and the two men stepped out of the way to let a nurse pushing a man in a wheelchair out before stepping inside.

Austin jabbed the number five with his knuckle. "I'm really looking forward to the slower pace in Jasper Creek."

"I dunno. It seemed pretty busy this week."

Austin gave him a curious look.

"Setting up for the Halloween festival."

"Right." Austin nodded. "I went last year. It was pretty fun."

Jackson bristled at the thought of Austin spending time with Anais.

"My girlfriend wasn't a fan though."

Discrete as ever, Anais hadn't mentioned Austin was seeing someone. The tightness in Jackson's chest loosened a little, his jealousy calming.

Austin frowned. "Well, ex-girlfriend now."

The green monster roared back to life in a flash.

The elevator dinged and the doors opened. Jackson followed Austin silently down the hallway, trying not to think of all the ways he could hurt him and make it look like an accident in a hospital. There were all sorts of things he could trip over or bump into or . . .

Before he could put any serious thought into his ridiculous ideas, Austin stopped in front of one of the many doors lining the hallway and knocked. Dr. Heather Miller was written on the placard on the door.

"Come in."

Anais's mother was sitting at her desk, typing at her computer when the two men walked in. She held up a hand and gestured for them to wait.

"Give me just one minute to finish this report." Her hands flew over the keyboard, then with a definitive tap, she nodded, and pushed her chair back to stand up.

"Oh, hello, Austin." She smiled first at him, then turned her sharp eyes to Jackson. "Nice to see you again, Jackson."

"I ran into him downstairs. Thought I'd stop by and say hello." Austin gave a wave. "So, hello. And goodbye."

"No, wait, Austin, I think you may be able to help." She kept her eyes on Jackson. "If you don't mind?"

It would be easy to say yes, he did mind, that this was private, and he didn't want Dr. Big Teeth hearing all about his broken hand. But the whole reason he was there was to get help, and if Dr. Miller thought Dr. Gibson could help, then who was he to argue?

Also, he didn't want it getting back to Anais that he'd been snotty with Austin. It felt like a weakness, or like he didn't trust her if he stayed jealous of her friend after she'd reassured him nothing was going on.

"It's fine."

Dr. Miller sat down and gestured for them to do the same.

"Now, why don't you walk me through what you need."

It was nothing to be embarrassed about, he knew. Athletes got hurt all the time. The hamate fracture he had was a relatively common one, and the surgery to fix it wasn't that complex. What was embarrassing was how long he'd waited to ask for help. Both with the initial fracture that had happened a few weeks before when he'd managed to push through until the end of the game before telling anyone, and, when faced with a scheduling snafu, he'd hesitated to reach out to his network to move things along.

It felt too much like his parents, using their connections to get invitations, special prices, all sorts of things. He was proud that he'd gotten drafted based on his talents, and not because his parents had made a call or were friends with a team owner or something. It was all done on his own, and to need help now at this crucial stage in his career felt like a betrayal of all of that.

"It's just a scheduling issue." He shifted in his seat, the eyes of both doctors on him. "I was supposed to have surgery ten days ago to remove a fractured hamate hook. But it got cancelled because—"

"Dr. Gartner had that golfing accident, that's right," Austin said, and Jackson bit the inside of his cheek to stop from saying something rude.

I'm here for help.

Dr. Miller sat back in her chair. "It definitely threw the team calendar into chaos for a while. What does Cassidy say about how things are now?"

Austin shifted in his chair. This must be why Dr. Miller had asked him to stay—he knew Cassidy. "We, uh, haven't spoken in a while."

There was a heavy pause as silence filled the room. Dr.

Miller's face hadn't moved, but her eyes had crinkled. Jackson might not have finished college, but it didn't take a genius to put the pieces together. Cassidy was Austin's ex-girlfriend, and Dr. Miller hadn't known that. He could also tell she desperately wanted to ask Austin about it, but couldn't, since Jackson was there.

Jackson cleared his throat. "I keep calling and no one seems to be able to tell me when I can have a new date." The words were thick in his throat, like they didn't want to come out. "My situation is still uncertain for next season, and the team isn't pushing for a new date. I've decided to pay for it myself, so I don't know if that's slowed things down even more."

"I'm sure it's just a mix-up. I'll give them a call right now." Dr. Miller picked up the phone.

Heat filled Jackson's face. "Thank you, ma'am."

She waved away his thanks. "You should have said something at family game night."

He shifted again, his eyes on her desk, the dark wood polished to a shine he could almost see himself in. "Well, ma'am, it was still scheduled then."

"Stop it with the ma'am. You can call me Heather." She flashed him a smile that was familiar. "We missed you these past few weeks."

She said it in the most offhand, polite way, but there was still sincerity in her eyes that did funny things to his chest. She had the same green eyes as Anais, which didn't help, even if hers were bracketed by laugh lines and covered in glasses.

"You went to family game night?" Austin asked quietly, as Dr. Miller spoke on the phone to someone.

Jackson shrugged. "Yeah."

"They've never invited me."

A lightness filled Jackson's chest.

Austin leaned back. "I didn't realize you were so close to . . . Bastien."

The question was there, Jackson could hear it in his voice. Was it just Bastien that Jackson was close to, or was it Anais as well?

He met the other man's eyes. They were tired, to be sure, but there was also sadness.

"It must be nice to have such good friends," Austin said quietly, almost to himself.

In an instant, all jealousy evaporated from Jackson. Whatever was going on with Austin, it had nothing to do with him. If the other man envied him for something like family game night, then he might be in the same kind of situation as Jackson. He didn't like to assume, but clearly there was a deep loneliness in Austin that he hid from everybody, even from Anais. She wouldn't even think to look for it, having always been surrounded by so much love from family and friends. Jackson only recognized it because it was so familiar to him.

"It'll be good for you to be in Jasper Creek, then." Jackson nodded. "The town loves their doctors."

Austin gave him a halfhearted smile, then sat back in his chair when Dr. Miller hung up the phone. In an instant, his face had smoothed out, and he was the same flawless man that everyone probably expected him to be.

"Well, I've got you a new appointment, Jackson."

His eyes shot back to Dr. Miller. "It was that easy?"

"Well, no, I had to promise a few things in exchange."

"I'm sorry, you shouldn't have to do that just for me—"

She held up a hand. "You've done so much for Bastien these past few weeks, it's the least I can do. And I didn't really have to promise much. Besides, there was a cancellation for tomorrow, so if you can pop down to billing right now, then they can review all the payment details with you."

His stomach churned to think at how much it would cost without insurance, but he knew it would be worth it long-term. Any money he spent was an investment in his future—and in Madison's. With the shorter recuperation period the surgery required, he'd be back to playing by January and ready for spring training. He just had to hope that would be enough to either keep his team interested or get another team's attention.

"Thank you so much, Dr. Miller." He stood and held out his hand. She took it in both of hers and gave him a warm smile that was so much like Anais, his breath caught in his lungs.

He held out his hand to Austin as well, who raised his eyebrows before shaking it.

"You two stay and visit. I can find my way back to the elevators," Jackson said.

He walked down the hall, a sense of relief replacing his earlier anxiety at being in a hospital. It wasn't what he thought he'd be doing when he got up that morning. But the more he thought about his conversation in the parking lot with Anais, the more he realized he had to do whatever he could to get what he wanted. She had such a clear vision of her perfect life, and it didn't include someone like him. The uncertainty of his life, the constant moving around, wasn't what she wanted. He'd been looking for a way to decide between baseball and Anais, but she'd already made the choice for him.

He pushed the elevator button gently.

This was for Madison more than anyone else. She was stuck, with no way out other than what Jackson could provide. The call had been heartbreaking, and he couldn't believe he'd let so much time go by without trying to schedule another surgery date. It had been the distraction of Anais, the fun of it. He'd gotten swept away.

Luckily, she had him firmly classified in the temporary category. The same organized and logical mind that he found so ridiculously attractive was the thing that kept her from seeing him as someone more permanent.

The elevator doors dinged, and he headed out into the atrium, feeling hopeful about the surgery, but depressed about Anais. It wasn't worth it to tell her, since it didn't change his plans to leave in a few days. She'd be out of his life, and he'd just be a blip to think back on fondly once she'd started her real life in Boston.

NINETEEN
ANAIS

When Anais walked into the Centennial University Hospital, she only had two things on her mind: margaritas and nachos.

The twice-monthly dinners Anais had with some of the doctors at CUH was a recent addition to her schedule that started by accident. Her mom had gotten a flat tire one day, and Anais volunteered to drive out to Denver to pick her up. Her dad could have done it, of course, but Elias had something going on at school that night, and he wasn't sure if he'd be back in time. Since it was the end of the day, her mom suggested they get something to eat before making the drive home. A few of her friends were also heading out at the same time, and her mom invited them along.

Anais smiled and nodded at familiar faces as she walked through the atrium of CUH, her mind still on the memory of that first dinner. Initially, she'd been irritated that her mom would rather have her friends there than spend it one-on-one with her daughter. In the end, it was an incredible evening and they decided to make it a regular event. She hadn't realized how much she needed to have a group of women professionals to share some of her thoughts and concerns with.

Isabelle was an amazing friend, but when Anais shared her work concerns, all she could do was listen and nod, and offer to punch annoying people in the face. It was the same thing Anais did when her friend vented about the stress of running the bar with her brother. Anais had friends from med school, of course, and Austin was close by if she needed to gripe to someone outside her family about her dad.

It was just . . . different when it was a group of women doctors. One was her mom's age, another closer to Anais's age, and both were resources in a world that was still not entirely easy for women to be in. Anais was a little spoiled out in Jasper Creek, but even in a town that loved her, there would always be people who asked to see her dad rather than her.

She didn't take it personally, since the most important thing was for a patient to be comfortable with their doctor, but it did sting in a way only these women could understand.

The cocktails and appetizers they ate during their dinners helped ease the sting as well.

After another long day dealing with the leftovers of the flu that had swept through Jasper Creek the previous week, Anais was focused on food and took the familiar route from the door to the elevator to her mother's office without paying much attention to her surroundings. Looking around absentmindedly, she did a double take when she saw Jackson Hart staring at her from across the hospital atrium, his eyes wide with shock. She made her way toward him, but he didn't move from his spot by the elevators.

"Hello," she said when she reached him, warmth creeping over her cheeks. Thoughts of margaritas and nachos were replaced by the memory of the last time they'd been together, in the parking lot by town square. The heat spread to her lips, aching for another kiss, when moments before they'd been wishing for melted cheese.

"What are you doing here?" The accusation in Jackson's voice cooled her down instantly.

"Meeting my mom." She put her hands on her hips, her lie detector on high alert. "What are you doing here?"

"Nothing."

"Are you alright?"

"Yes."

The silence that settled between them was tense and awkward. She knew he was hiding something, and she wanted to demand he tell her what it was.

Except they weren't a couple, they weren't anything other than two people who kissed. A lot. With more passion and heat Anais had ever thought possible. Still, there was no rule that they had to be honest with each other, even though he'd been sharing bits of his past with her over the past few weeks. This is what the logical part of Anais was telling her.

The emotional part of Anais—the one she tried to pretend she didn't have—was hurt beyond belief.

"Why are you lying to me?"

Jackson ran a hand through his hair, his gaze hovering right over her shoulder. "I'm not lying. It's just not something I want to talk about with you."

"Wow." She stepped back and dropped her hands. "You don't want to talk about a medical issue with me. A doctor."

"No, that's not—I mean, you're not—" He sighed and ran a hand along the back of his beck.

Fire crept slowly through her veins. She knew exactly how he wanted to finish that sentence. How so many men had thought of her over the years. She was either one thing or the other to them, a woman who'd let her own career fall by the wayside for theirs, or a doctor with zero trace of romantic potential. The stupid hope she'd been nursing the past week was all because Jackson had seemed like he saw her as both.

Looks like I was wrong. It didn't happen often, and when it did, it was usually a code-red-level mistake.

Anais shifted to professional doctor mode, erasing any trace of jealous not-really-his-girlfriend from her voice. "Does this have anything to do with why next season is up in the air?"

He inhaled and twisted his lips, like he didn't want to answer. Eventually, he nodded.

"That didn't seem like something worth talking to me about?"

"What difference would it have made?" His eyes narrowed. "You're going to Boston."

"For a year, not the rest of my life." She wanted to throw up her hands, but even fired up, she was conscious that she was having this conversation—this fight—with Jackson in the middle of the hospital where countless people who knew her would see. She kept them balled at her sides. "I thought that with things so uncertain, it meant that you might not be playing anymore."

His eyes grew wide. "What?"

"You said the other day, things were unsettled for next season."

"That doesn't mean I'd stop playing." He shook his head. "I can't stop playing. Why would I?"

The words came to her right away, but she stopped them on her lips before she could really embarrass herself.

Because of me.

Embarrassed tears pricked at her eyes and she blinked them away. Had she really been so stupid to think that what her parents had was possible for her? Maybe it only worked for a superwoman like her mom. Someone like Anais just wasn't enough. The quiet life she wanted would never be what anyone else wanted. Not someone like Jackson, who was caring and strong, and, up until that point, had seemed the opposite of every egotistical doctor she'd dated and every career-obsessed athlete Bastien had ever introduced her to.

How she could be so wrong was baffling.

Logic was her foundation, and she grabbed hold of it like a falling woman did a rope. "If you're injured, then you can't keep playing."

"I won't be injured in a few more days." He gestured around. "That's why I'm here. So I can keep playing for a long time."

"That's what you really want." She was proud her voice didn't waver. There was no trace of the pain cutting through her chest.

"Yes, Anais, is that surprising? It's what your brother wanted. He'd trade anything for a chance to play professionally."

Anais sucked in a breath. She knew Bastien was unhappy, but she hadn't thought it was that bad. He was busy with teaching and helping around town, enjoying life in a way that Anais never allowed herself. He was out all the time having fun, while she was the responsible one, carrying on family tradition, thinking of the future of Miller Family Medical.

The one time she let herself indulge in something fun, something reckless, it was blowing up in her face and tearing her heart out.

"Well then, I hope you feel better soon. I'm sure I'll hear from Bastien how it goes, since I'm the last person you'll talk to about it."

It wasn't what she wanted to say. What she wanted to do was cry, and ask him why he was trading a chance with her for his career.

But she already knew why.

She tossed her hair and walked past him toward the elevators. His hand wrapped around her arm, pulling her back.

"Wait, Anais, I'm not—"

"Don't." She shook his hand off.

It would be too easy to let him apologize. He was too tempting to let him keep talking. Her defenses were already so low against him, it wouldn't take much. She had to save herself from more hurt, from the story he was sure to tell her. A story she'd heard before, where giving up everything for him would somehow be worth it so they could be together.

A story she'd never wanted for herself.

He wasn't meant for her, she'd known that from the beginning. Her real chance at love was somewhere in Boston, someone who would see her for everything she was. She thought Jackson had. Clearly she'd been mistaken. For him to keep something like this from her, something medical, something impacting his career in a major way, impacting their possible future together . . . It was proof he only wanted a tiny piece of her, the only piece that he'd seen.

Deciding to take the stairs instead of waiting for the elevator, she hurried off without looking back. Her feet hit the floor at a fast enough pace it was clear she didn't want him following, but not so fast it looked like she was running away. When their encounter started circulating around CUH, she didn't want them to say that Dr. Miller had been running away from anything.

Even if that was exactly what she wanted to do.

TWENTY

ANAIS

When Anais opened the door to the stairway on the fifth floor, her eyes were dry. The walk had done her good, the fight or flight response to a perceived danger having been satisfied by the movement, and the cortisol should be working its way out of her system. Her body could relax, and the stress response she'd had to the fight wouldn't impact her night.

It was therefore as surprising to her as it was to her mom that the second they caught sight of each other in the long hallway, Anais burst into tears.

Dr. Heather Miller wasn't the one her children ran to when they were upset. That had always been their dad, the one with big, warm arms to hug away whatever pain his unrelenting vigilance had been unable to protect them from. The Miller matriarch's role was one of teacher, scholar, and disciplinarian. Comfort did not come easily to Heather.

That didn't stop Anais's mom from putting her arms around her daughter and gently rubbing her back.

"Goodness, I guess we'd better get you some nachos, stat."

Anais let out a blubbery laugh. Food was the main way her mom showed love, for sure.

The other women were waiting in the employee parking lot, which was thankfully accessible without passing through the atrium. Even if Jackson was long gone, she didn't want to return to the scene of embarrassment and start crying all over again.

It was a quick drive to the tapas bar the women favored for their evenings, and Anais used the time to dry her eyes.

"Do you want to talk about it?" her mom asked before they went into the restaurant.

Anais shook her head. "Not yet."

"Hmm." Her mom gave her one of her piercing looks. "You'll change your mind after a few margaritas."

It only took one for the whole story to come tumbling out of her. Meeting Jackson at the bar before she knew who he was, the kiss in the basement during family game night, the trips out to see Aunt Deb, their mutual decision to keep things light and fun while he was in town, then finally, the fight in the hospital.

The three doctors around the table didn't hesitate to launch into diagnosis mode, probing for more details.

"If this was something fun and light, why does it matter if he didn't tell you about his injury?" Yvonne, a pulmonologist with tight curls and a nose piercing, had her head in her hand and was looking at Anais like she was a difficult case of pneumonia.

"Well, if he might not play anymore, that's important information to know before diving into something like this."

"Why?" Zariah was a radiologist and had two little girls at home. Her deep-brown eyes were crinkled with curiosity.

"Because then it's not really just light and fun, is it? It could be something more."

"It could still be something more, even if he plays." Her mom crunched into a nacho. She'd taken the news that Anais had kissed someone in her basement without even a flinch. All the years of pressure to be the perfect daughter felt like a lie Anais had been telling herself.

"I don't see how. He'll be off playing, I'll be in Boston. It would never work. Not the way it did for you and dad."

Her mom sighed and folded her arms across her chest. "You hold us up like the perfect marriage sometimes, but it's not really like that."

"I know, I know, you fight like anybody else." Anais waved her hand. "But you never had to sacrifice your career, and he always supported you. Why should I expect any less?"

Yvonne and Zariah nodded in agreement. Their own partners were of the same mold, moving all over the country to follow them and being the stay-at-home dads their wives' demanding careers needed.

"I've sacrificed plenty, Anais, and so have Yvonne and Zariah."

More nodding.

"Wait, what?" Anais blinked at the three of them.

"It's not about someone being totally subservient and doing whatever you want."

"That's not what I thought it was." Or maybe it had been, a little. Everything was so black and white for Anais. It was either her career or theirs. She had to live in Jasper Creek, and no other town would do. Even her neat little categorization of ice cream and movies, a silly game, came from a place of needing to control and predict the world around her.

"Those first years when I was still finishing school and your dad was in Colorado were hard. I pushed myself to the limit, skipped parties and hanging out so that I could finish a year early and start medical school sooner." Her mom grabbed another nacho. "I could have transferred right away to something closer to him, but I was at a state school, and my parents could cover the entire cost. That was also important, so we wouldn't have tons of debt right off the bat as a married couple. Do you know why I chose radiology?"

Anais pushed at the nacho on her plate, crushing it into tiny pieces. "You said it was what you always wanted to do."

"It was, once I met your dad. But I grew up wanting to be a surgeon and didn't think I'd ever get married or have kids."

The revelation struck Anais in the chest hard. Dinner wasn't going the way it usually did. While there was always career advice or insider tips from her mom to the others on the politics of working in a hospital, this was the first time she was hearing so much about the early days and decisions with her dad.

The other two women, however, looked as though they were already aware of all of this.

"I matched to a few different specialties, and I took my second choice so that I could live in a cheaper city where my husband could find a job," Yvonne said. "He still would have moved wherever I ended up, but I didn't want it to be hard for him either."

Zariah nodded. "I say no to things all the time, so that I can be home in time to help put the girls to bed." She raised a glass. "I say yes to the things that matter the most. That's what balance is. Not forcing everything on one person all the time."

"That's not what I think Mom does." Anais took a large gulp of her drink as a wave of unease washed over her. These women usually understood her so well, but this wasn't the same thing as a husband who was a software engineer or wanting to have a night off to hang out with friends.

Jackson was a freaking baseball player. There'd be no kind of balance at all, no chance at the kind of life Anais wanted. He didn't even want to try, wasn't even considering it, based on everything he'd been keeping from her. He knew there was no shot. So she shouldn't even be upset.

"Do you know why your dad did that fellowship in Boston?" her mom said, leaning her elbows on the table.

Anais blinked. "It's where his dad studied, and his grandad. It's what Millers do."

"Your grandad basically forced him to go. Your dad never wanted it. He was happy in Jasper Creek with his girlfriend, and he was going to propose."

"I thought she dumped him."

"She did, for a neurologist from Denver. He was a mess when I met him." Her mom shook her head and chuckled, then took a sip from her drink. "He thought doing the fellowship would impress her, even though he didn't want to go. Once he was there, he was super focused on it and wouldn't even consider any other possibility." She raised an eyebrow.

Anais just barely avoided rolling her eyes as the very obvious reference to her own single-mindedness about her goals. "Dad always said I got my stubbornness from you." With the sulkiness of her teenage brother, she shoved some nachos into her mouth.

It had been her mom's stubbornness, after all, that had kept her shy, awkward dad from leaving the bar that night without getting a promise he'd call her. Now she saw that familiar story in a new light. Her dad hadn't even wanted to be in Boston. He'd been thinking of someone else, of some other life when he'd met her mom. It could have turned into nothing, but one of them had seen the possibility of more and decided to hold on.

"Speaking of stubbornness, have you seen that new overtime rule the board is pushing through?" Zariah turned the topic away from Anais's personal drama and onto hospital drama, leaving her free to brood over this new information.

Millers had always done these fellowships, but her dad hadn't wanted to. Is that why he was pushing so hard for her to stay? Because he didn't want her to feel the pressure his father had put on him?

She had to smile around a mouthful of chips and cheese. He really was a great dad.

Still, his situation had been totally different. He'd thought he'd found love in Jasper Creek before his heart had been broken. Bastien had gone through something similar with Brenda. Maybe it wasn't that the men in town weren't interested in Anais, but more that she'd been predisposed to mistrust any of them who showed interest. The Millers didn't have a great track record, after all. Her mom's point seemed to be that Anais's plan to do things the way her parents had, the way Millers were expected to, wasn't necessarily as clear cut of a route as she'd thought.

Figuring out how this new vision of love and life fit into the carefully planned path she'd set for herself would take some time. It probably wasn't best to do this kind of thinking with her mother's eagle eyes staring at her from across the table while she listened to hospital gossip. Anais would have the drive back to Jasper Creek on her own to mull things over.

Jackson was a whole separate issue. They weren't a couple, they weren't anything, and he'd be gone in a few days. There was no way anything could work for them.

"You're looking awfully pensive over there." Yvonne reached out and squeezed her hand. "All you really have to do is decide what you want. And since we know you're like both your mom and your dad, once you figure it out, you'll figure out a way to get it."

Her mom had her most patient smile on her face. "What do you want, Anais?"

The churning in her stomach was as unfamiliar as the feeling of Jackson being mad at her gave her. For the first time in a long time, Anais wasn't sure what she wanted.

Well, except one thing.

"I want more nachos, please."

TWENTY-ONE
JACKSON

It should have been a good day. He had a new surgery date. Phil was going to let the team know, and he'd push to get a final answer about next season. This was what Jackson wanted. The tightness in his chest on the drive back to Jasper Creek shouldn't have been there.

When he walked into Bastien's house, he found his friend on all fours on the ground, hammering something. Technically all threes, since he had his hurt arm tucked up against his chest.

"What are you doing?" He put the keys onto the hook by the door. When he first arrived at Bash's house, the keys were always hard to find, on a table somewhere, or in a pants pocket in the laundry. The hook had taken Jackson less than five minutes to install, and he felt good knowing even when he left Jasper Creek in a few days, his friend's life would still be a little easier thanks to him.

Unfortunately, it didn't seem to be easy at the moment.

"I'm finishing this sign for the festival."

"Why didn't you wait for me?" He'd texted to let Bastien know it would take longer than planned at the hospital. The meeting with the very patient lady in billing had taken forever.

In part because it turned out she was a baseball fan and had asked Jackson endless questions. It had been nice, actually, like it had been with Elias and his friends the other night. Seeing others love the game made him want to keep playing even more.

Only the memory of Anais's disappointed face made him wish he loved the game a little less.

"I didn't think it would take so long. I thought I'd be done by the time you got back." Bastien exhaled heavily and sat back on his knees, using his shirt to wipe the sweat off his brow. "I might have taken on a bit more than I should have."

"You think?" Jackson tried to chuckle, but it came out hollow. Bastien's dedication to the town, his aim for perfectionism, reminded him too much of Anais. He thought the twins were so different, but at their heart, they wanted the same thing. To do right by their family and their town. The realization struck him in the chest, and he felt even more like a jerk for what had happened at the hospital with Anais.

"Why is it so important for the festival to go well?"

"I told you why." Bastien held out his hand, and Jackson helped him to his feet. He moved slowly to the couch and flopped down onto it. "It's important tourism money. The town's reputation."

Jackson sat down next to him. "Yeah, but like, why is it important for you?"

Bastien shrugged and frowned. "Geez, I dunno, Jack, it just is. Why's baseball so important to you?"

"Because of Madison."

Bastien blinked in surprise. Jackson had never told him that. "What does baseball have to do with your little sister?"

"I want to be able to pay for her school, whatever she wants to do, so she doesn't have to rely on my parents."

Saying it out loud to a friend was a relief after so many years of keeping it to himself. It was fine for people to think he only cared about the money and the fame, but after the fight with Anais, he was worried that's what everyone thought about him.

"Wow." Bastien nodded slowly. "That makes way more sense than you're just a shallow jackass like I'd been assuming this whole time."

Jackson laughed, a real one this time. He slapped Bastien on the back and went to get them a couple of beers from the fridge. When he got back to the couch, Bastien was looking thoughtful again, his phone in his hand.

"Uh oh, what's that look about?" Jackson sat down and handed him a bottle. "I'm not taking you to the Floodline tonight, even if you beg."

Bastien shook his head. "Just realizing now why this surgery is so important to you."

"It's not just for my career. It's for Maddy too."

"But it means nothing will be possible with Anais."

The bottle in Jackson's hand froze halfway to his lips. A drop of condensation fell onto his hand while panic dripped down his neck. He took a slow sip, then placed the bottle carefully down on the coffee table. "What does that mean?"

Bastien cast him a wry look. "It means, idiot, that I know you two have a thing going on."

"Since when?"

Bastien rolled his eyes. "Since Matt Hayes told me he saw you at the Floodline on free ice-cream day."

"You've known this whole time?"

Bash shrugged. "Yeah."

"But . . . " Jackson ran a shaky hand through his hair. Bash was way too calm. "But you told me not to flirt with her that night at her house."

"Yeah, well, that was before Matt told me how happy Anais looked talking to you." Bash looked down at his bottle like it contained all the answers in the world.

Jackson picked up his beer again and took a long sip, wondering where this was going. Bash didn't seem mad that they'd been . . . well, whatever he'd been with Anais. But he didn't seem happy about it, either.

"Look." Jackson set the bottle down with a clunk on the table, his hand still wrapped around it. "Our thing was just a vacation fling, no big deal. And anyway, it's over."

"What? Just like that?"

Jackson thought back to the look of hurt on Anais's face when she realized why he was at the hospital. When she realized everything he'd been keeping from her.

"Yeah. I'm leaving once the surgery is done."

"So? You could still see her."

It was too weird, to have Bash pushing for the very thing Jackson had been terrified he'd be pissed about. "How? She's about to spend a year in Boston, and I'm this close to getting my shot at the majors."

"But what if you don't make it?"

The panic was back, red-hot and tinged with anger.

"Gee, thanks for believing in me."

"I'm not trying to be a jerk. I just mean, like, what's your plan for after? You can't play forever."

It was the same question Jackson had been asking himself since he got to Jasper Creek. "I don't know, okay?" He stood, pacing up and down Bastien's small living room, suddenly too hot for this conversation. "I have zero skills, no degree, and absolutely nothing to offer her."

Jackson stopped and turned to see Bastien smirking from him on the couch.

"You don't have to offer her anything. She's not into guys for money. Or looks."

Jackson ignored the dig. "Of course she's into money. Everyone is."

"Maybe in your world. We're a long way from Charleston out here."

Through the haze of his swirling temper, a part of Jackson realized it was true. There was nothing flashy about Jasper Creek, nothing about the Millers that reminded him of his parents. Other than the doctor thing. Which, he also realized, he had been a judgmental jerk about.

"Aw, hell, I really messed up, didn't I?"

He flopped back onto the couch and put his head in his hands. Bastien gave him a rough thump on the shoulder.

"Probably. But she's kind of used to screwups, in case you hadn't noticed." Bastien indicated his leg and arm. "So are you going to tell her you *like* like her, or do I have to pass her a note that says 'Will you go out with Jackson, circle yes or no'?"

"What would be the point?" Jackson rubbed his hands across his face. "She's still going to Boston."

Bastien blinked. "Oh shoot, I think I know why she picked Boston."

"What do you mean? She said the women's health experience will help the town." He gave Bastien a significant look. "Because apparently that's all you Millers think about."

"That's the reason she gave to my parents too." Bastien scratched his chin. "But it doesn't have to be Boston. I'm sure she could have found something closer."

"So what's in Boston?" His heart gave a jealous thud against his chest.

"It's where my dad met my mom. You've seen them together. They're like this perfect couple."

Something rumbled in Jackson's stomach. Anais was all about plans and order and knowing what happens next. It was reassuring to someone like Jackson, who liked the same kind of predictability. Even if he'd chosen a career that had way less certainty, he was still in control of most of it. In control of his discipline, his performance, his body. The past weeks without it, without knowing about the surgery or the future of his contract, had been torture.

Bastien was shaking his head. "It totally makes sense now. She thinks that's where she'll find someone, since no one in town has ever been interested in her."

"This town must be full of idiots, then."

"Millers almost never marry people from Jasper Creek. We bring them back here. It's kind of our thing."

"Well, isn't that cute." It should be fine with him that she'd end up with someone else. He would have his career and the life he wanted for his sister.

Bash had a sad smile on his face. "You know, that's part of why I was so bummed about not being able to play soccer. I always thought I'd meet someone and bring them back here when I was done playing."

"You don't hate it here?"

"Of course not. I just struggle with the same thing Anais does. I've known everyone my entire life. I thought at first that was a good thing, but then Brenda—" He stopped himself, a painful look crossing his face.

Jackson put an arm on his shoulder. "She didn't deserve you, man."

"Do you deserve Anais?"

"What?" He pulled his hand away. "You're talking like this is still a possibility. Like she doesn't totally hate me now for not telling her about the surgery."

"I thought you didn't even want to do it anymore until you told me you were going to Denver today." Bastien leaned back on the couch. "I figured you didn't ask my mom for help to get a new surgery date because you wanted to spend more time here with Anais."

"That's not why. It's because . . . "

Wait, was that why he'd been putting it off? Yes, there was his intense dislike of hospitals and doctors, and not wanting to use his connections to get special treatment. Had all that just been an excuse?

Maybe the real reason he hadn't told her about his hand was because then she'd be the one to help him fix it. Then she'd be the one to push him away, when she realized how much trouble he was. Just like his parents.

She's never rejected her brother for needing help . . .

Things were getting clearer, but not everything bouncing around in his brain made sense, not fully, not yet. He still had to work some things out, and there was still time to do it. He just had to figure out what he wanted.

TWENTY-TWO
ANAIS

Even though she looked forward to it every year, Anais woke up on the first morning of the Halloween festival without even the slightest inclination to go. It had been another long, sleepless night pondering over the conversation with her mom, Yvonne, and Zariah. What had seemed like a simple and clear path forward a few days before was now uncertain, based on faulty logic. It might not even be what she really wanted.

That didn't mean she knew what she *actually* wanted. The time alone in the car ride home hadn't helped anything. The midnight rewatch of season three of *The Tudors* probably hadn't helped, either.

The thought of going to the festival didn't fill her with anything other than dread. Either Jackson would be there and not talk to her, or he wouldn't be there because he'd already left. There was no way of knowing, so there was no way of preparing herself. To let herself imagine one scenario sent her heart rate pulsing, then the other possibility slammed into her, and she would sweat with anxiety and blubber with sadness.

For someone who was all about making plans and following through on them, this was a completely unfamiliar situation to be in. It was beyond uncomfortable, almost painful. Over-whelmed with choices, her brain settled into old, comforting patterns. The easiest thing would be to stay inside, watch *Enola Holmes* for the fourth time, and remind herself that she was much luckier than women back in the nineteenth century.

Isabelle Hayes, however, had other ideas.

"Why aren't you dressed yet?" Isabelle let herself into the house at ten in the morning to find Anais sitting in her pajamas eating Rocky Road in front of the TV.

Only slightly embarrassed, Anais shoved another spoonful in her mouth and gave a halfhearted shrug. "I don't think I'll go."

"I'm sorry, what's that? A Miller opting out of a town event?"

Anais set her bowl down on the coffee table and leaned back on the couch. "The town won't crumble beneath us if there are only six instead of seven of us there today."

Isabelle sat down next to her and put her hand to Anais's forehead. "Are you feeling alright?"

She squirmed out of reach. "I'm fine. What's the big deal if I don't go?"

Instead of a snappy reply, Isabelle actually paused to consider. "We'd have people asking us for weeks why we didn't go."

"We don't have to answer. It's none of their business." Anais crossed her arms over her chest and stuck out her lower lip. For once in her life, she was going to be just as childish as all of her siblings and let them sort things out.

Isabelle leaned her head on Anais's shoulder. "Did some-thing happen with Jackson?"

A sharp stab in her stomach caught Anais off guard. "What?"

"Don't think you can fool me. You've been all smiley and mysterious ever since he got into town." Isabelle gave an exaggerated sigh and put her hands over her heart. "I can understand why. He's very dreamy."

"A dreamy liar is what he is."

Though she'd gotten plenty of advice the previous night from her mom and her colleagues, it was time for some best friend input. Even if she didn't always understand the doctor part of Anais's life, Isabelle knew more about love than anyone else. It must have something to do with working at a bar. Seeing people on dates, serving them drinks when they were upset or celebrating. People told Isabelle even more about their medical problems than they did Anais.

So out came the whole story. Apparently Jackson and Anais hadn't been as discreet as they thought they'd been, since the two of them had been frequent topics of discussion at the Floodline the past week.

"What are people saying?" she asked, not sure if she wanted to hear the answer or not. "And why aren't they saying anything to me directly?"

A tiny smirk on her face, Isabelle tilted her head to the side. "I thought it was none of their business?"

"It's not." The moment she said the words, Anais realized how true they were.

She'd been so worried about what the people in town thought. Starting on that first day in the café, all the eyes on them, her hands shaking from excited nerves at seeing him unexpectedly. Then again when he showed up at the office to get a prescription for Bastien, and all the patients in the waiting room witnessed the exchange. Even at the hospital, throughout the fight, she'd had the worry in the back of her mind that word would get back to Jasper Creek about their confrontation. The only person from town who worked there was her mom, but people would occasionally go there for procedures.

In the back of her mind, there was always the endless refrain. *What will people think?*

"It's not about what people think, it's about what I want for my life," she said out loud.

Her mom and the others had said as much over dinner, but Anais had been too worked up to let the words sink in. Of course they'd been right. Her mom was always right.

Isabelle grabbed a chip from the open bag on the table and crunched into it. "So, do you want to go to the Halloween festival?"

Anais really thought about it, taking away the considerations of what people would or wouldn't say if she went. Did she enjoy the festival? Did she want to help Elias with his booth, because she actually had fun with her brother?

A smile spread across her face, and Isabelle cheered. "Excellent. I'll go pick out something cute for you to wear."

An hour later, they were walking into town square arm in arm in matching denim overalls. It wasn't quite Anais's definition of cute, but Isabelle had paired it with a flannel shirt tied at the waist and rolled up hems everywhere to make it look way more interesting than Anais could have managed. The looks she was getting weren't because of what she was wearing, but she tried to pretend they were. It would be easier than the alternative, that everyone was wondering about her and Jackson.

Or maybe they're just happy to see me here. They were smiling, after all.

"He might not even be here," she whispered to Isabelle as they waved at people passing by.

"You're not here for him. You're here for you, remember?"

Anais took a deep breath. Doing things for herself. That was what this was about. It didn't solve the larger question of what to do about the fellowship and Jackson, but at least for today, she could focus on one thing. That was the only plan she needed: enjoy the festival she waited all year for.

It was easy enough to do that, with her favorite fall colors and smells surrounding her. Before they went to the baseball team's booth, Anais and Isabelle stopped for a donut from Carlie and her grandad, Carl Sr.—this year's special festival flavor was pistachio cream—a caramel apple from another booth, and then browsed the stacks at the Odd Page Books tent.

"When are you going to tell me what's going on with Tina?" Anais whispered to Isabelle when the owner of the bookshop caught sight of Isabelle and started flushing immediately.

"Soon." Isabelle had a little private smile on her face. "You're not the only one who doesn't like to talk about love until it's further along."

Anais let out a shocked chuckle. "Love? That's not what I feel for Jackson."

"Isn't that why this whole thing is so hard?" Isabelle gave her a knowing look.

Leaving her with that terrifyingly exciting thought, Isabelle wandered out of the book tent, blowing a kiss at Tina as she left. Anais gripped the worn copy of *Stardust* in her hands, her friend's words tumbling around in her head.

Another piece of the conversation with her mother finally sunk in. What had happened between Anais's mom and dad had been too strong to ignore, even though it made no sense for either of them at the time. They'd both already chosen their paths, and it didn't include someone like the person they'd met that night. They'd made it work, because it wasn't supposed to be easy, but it was easy to decide to do the work when you believed it would be worth it.

Anais had brushed the comparison away because the

circumstances were so different. She wasn't a twenty-year-old pre-med student sneaking into a bar to hear her favorite band. Jackson wasn't a shy, awkward doctor from a small town in Colorado out for a night with friends. Her dad would have let love slip away if her mom hadn't decided he was the one for her and nothing would stop them from being together.

Anais certainly wasn't the powerhouse that her mom was. Sure, she had that same stubborn, determined streak, but she was also a homebody, like her dad. Nothing made her happier than being in Jasper Creek, surrounded by friends and family. The only reason she'd considered leaving for a year was because her dad had done it.

Was that just something else she was doing for others, and not what she actually wanted? She'd been drawn to women's health as a specialty, and it would absolutely help their practice. Except every time she went to visit her mom at work, her first thought was always, "I'm so glad to be done with hospitals." Another year in one wouldn't be the worst thing ever, but at what cost to her own happiness?

There were other ways to get that kind of expertise besides her doing something that, in her heart, she really didn't want to do. She'd been away long enough during medical school and residency. She wanted to stay. Her dad wasn't pushing her to do it the way her grandad had pushed him. It really was entirely up to her if she went to Boston or not.

A shout from a kid running through the booths pulled her out of her thoughts. She checked her watch and realized that if she was going to help Elias, it should be sooner rather than later.

When she got to the booth, her dad was already there, helping her youngest brother count money and hand out prizes to the lucky kids with a preternaturally accurate fastball. Anais walked behind the booth and put her hands over her dad's shoulders, hugging him tightly.

"What's this about?" He turned and hugged her back. "Your mom said you might be feeling under the weather today, so I volunteered to pitch in. After all, I'll be the one to do it next year when you're away."

"Thanks, Dad." She gave him a squeeze, then took a deep breath. "I don't think I'll take the fellowship after all."

Happiness lit up his eyes. "Really? Are you sure that's what you want?" His smile turned faraway and nostalgic. "I didn't want to go at first, but I ended up having a great time in Boston."

"I know you did." She laughed.

"You are right that we need to specialize more."

"What if Austin still comes to work for us?"

Her dad tilted his head, considering this for a moment, then nodded. "I'll have to do some number crunching, but I think we could make it work."

"Great." That was at least one problem solved. Informing the fellowship could wait until Monday. It was still a risky move career-wise, but if there was anything she'd learned from all the margarita and nacho nights, it was that careers could take all different kinds of paths. Plus, she wasn't doing it last minute. There was enough time before her start date that the program could likely find someone else to take her spot, which would help smooth things over. It was much better for everyone to have a doctor invested in the program.

Speaking of doctors being invested in their program, she'd have to call Austin later to discuss her change in plans. It would be fun to work with him, but she wanted to hear the whole story about why he was so ready to leave CUH. While she knew it was probably just a string of broken hearts he was eager to get away from, she didn't want there to be the same kind of thing happening here. Clementine had seemed a little too excited to hear he'd be working in Jasper Creek in a few months, and she wouldn't be the only one once the news got around. Anais would need to lay down some rules for Austin. She still cared about her town, even if she was trying to put herself and what she needed first.

The afternoon at the booth with Elias was enjoyable, especially since she was there for the right reasons. Spending time with her youngest brother was something she enjoyed much more now that he was in high school. When she'd been a senior, he'd been an eight-year-old chatterbox bugging her constantly with his questions and running commentary on his newest Pokémon card. Now the ten-year age gap was more manageable, and his questions were geared toward picking a major and how to pass his pre-med classes.

Though she knew it would eventually come, it was still hard to hear the one question she didn't want him to ask.

"Hey, have you seen Jackson at all today?" Elias looked around eagerly. There was a break in visitors to the booth, and they were sipping on hot cider their dad had just brought over.

"Uh, no."

"He said he'd show me some drills to get more power into my hitting."

"He might have left already."

"Really?" Elias looked disappointed. "Well, I guess that's kind of what his life is like."

And there it was, in such a simple way, the crux of the problem Anais had with Jackson. Why he could never be a real possibility. She'd made her choice to stay in Jasper Creek, but there was no guarantee Jackson would ever want the same thing.

TWENTY-THREE
JACKSON

In the middle of the Halloween festival wasn't where Jackson wanted to have a serious conversation with Anais, but Bastien hadn't left him much of a choice. Since Bash knew how Jackson felt about Anais, it seemed his brotherly protective instinct was to ensure they got together.

"She might not want to talk to me," Jackson said for about the tenth time that morning as they walked through the crowds milling around the elementary school field. The rides looked pretty tame, but the kids were shrieking loud enough to drown out his grumbling to Bastien. "And what if she isn't even here?"

"She'll be here." Bastien shook hands with someone passing by. They'd been at the festival since six o'clock, making sure everything was set up. It had been a whirlwind morning, running back and forth between booths to deliver everything from extension cords to donuts. At least Jackson got a few free donuts for all his trouble. The thought of heading back into training and the stricter diet that required wasn't something Jackson was looking forward to. He wasn't looking forward to the surgery either, but he'd always made sacrifices to achieve his goals.

Was he willing to sacrifice Anais? That was the question he'd kept coming back to last night. The talk with Bash had ended without any firm next steps. Then they'd played video games for hours, giving time for Jackson's mind to wander and imagine all the possibilities.

If he managed to find her, he'd have to explain everything, lay it all out for her, in a way he never had before for any other woman. That in and of itself felt like a huge sacrifice, to reveal himself that way to someone. Even Bash didn't know every-thing. Telling him about Madison had helped Jackson see things differently. What if telling Anais more about his life would make her see him differently, but in a bad way?

As much as he wanted to find her, he wasn't completely upset that she hadn't shown up yet. The extra time to prepare was a relief, a chance to organize his thoughts and prepare his words.

But when he caught sight of her in the corner of his eye while delivering a new folding table to one of the booths, his stomach dropped. He wasn't ready. What if she said no? What if he laid everything out for her, and she found him lacking, just the way his parents did?

Deep breaths.

He'd survived their rejection. He could handle another. Hers would hurt even more, but he'd just have to get through it somehow. At the very least, he'd be able to rub it in Bash's face for the rest of his life. *Though I'll never be able to come back to Jasper Creek*, he realized sadly.

He liked it here. There was the natural beauty that surrounded the small town—Bastien had been right about that. It was quieter than Seattle, and closer knit than Charleston. Watching everyone the last few weeks, he saw that they were like a team. A really big one, that helped each other, and had fun with the competitive streak that ran through everyone, rather than turn it into something ugly.

It took another half hour of running around before Jackson had a break and could even think about heading over to the baseball team's booth. When he got there, however, there was just Elias and Dr. Miller sitting behind it.

"Hi, Jackson." Elias jumped up, excited to see him.

"Heya, E."

The teenager looked thrilled at the nickname.

Jackson nodded at Elias's dad, who nodded back. "Dr. Miller."

"Do you have time now to show me those drills?" Elias was already halfway out of the booth. "I have my bat in the car."

"Don't you have to finish up your shift here?" His eyes cut to Dr. Miller, who had an indulgent smile on his face, unlike anything Jackson had ever seen from his own parents.

"I can handle it. Anais will be back soon. She just went to grab more change from the middle school."

"I'll meet you at the lower field." Elias ran in the direction of the parking lot, leaving his dad and Jackson chuckling.

It wasn't what he'd planned, but it was still a break. He'd enjoyed helping Elias get ready for fall ball. It was nice to see the same enthusiasm he'd had as a kid. It reminded him of why he loved the game so much.

Also, the field was right next to the middle school, so he might luck out and catch Anais there. At least then it could be a more private conversation than in the middle of the festival.

By the time he got to the field, he knew he'd made the right choice. Anais was scolding Elias, a fierce expression on her face, when Jackson walked up.

"You can't just run off and leave Dad and me to do all the work." Her arms were folded tightly against her chest.

"Aw, come on, Nissy, Jackson's leaving soon. This might be my last chance to get his help."

Her eyes caught his just then, and something flickered across them. Hope soared in his chest. Was she sad that he would be leaving soon?

"I don't think we should take up any of Mr. Hart's time."

"It's fine." Jackson gave Elias a nod. "I like helping him."

"Alright then, I need to get back to the booth to help my dad." She avoided his eyes, then started to walk away.

"Wait." He glanced at Elias. "I'm not going anywhere this afternoon. Could you run these up to your dad so I can have a quick chat with Anais about something?"

Elias seemed pleased to get a direct request from Jackson, and he grabbed the bags from Anais's hand before she could protest.

"Be right back."

Jackson breathed in deeply, then let it out slowly. "I have about five minutes to get this all out before he's back."

"It's fine, you don't need to say anything." Anais lifted a hand to her forehead, but Jackson stepped closer and tucked her hair behind her ear for her, the brief contact with her skin sending a shiver of anticipation down his spine. The proximity to her was just as intoxicating as it had been that first night at the Floodline, maybe even more so. Now that he'd gotten to know her, had made this decision to try to have her in his life, every part of him seemed to ache for her.

If what she wanted wasn't him, he'd be okay with that. Not right away, but eventually.

"Can I tell you a story?"

She inhaled a shaky breath and nodded, her eyes flicking up to his before darting away.

"Once there was a little boy in Charleston who loved base-ball. He played it all the time. But his parents wanted him to be a doctor, like them. When he went away to college, they agreed to pay for it if he studied the things they wanted him to study."

Her lips turned down a little. He'd told her parts of this, but not the details.

"The boy got a scholarship to play baseball in California, so he didn't need their money. When he got offered a contract his junior year, he thought he'd never need their money again."

Her lips ticked up. "Did he make any friends while he was in California?"

"Yes, a very good friend, from Colorado, who he never got to visit until years later, but I'm getting ahead of myself." He took another breath. It wasn't too hard this way, to tell the story like it was about someone else. "This boy had a little sister, who he loved very much and was worried she'd have to become a doctor, too, even if she didn't want to. So when he got that contract, he promised her he'd save all his money so that she could have whatever life she wanted."

"Jackson, I didn't realize—"

He put a hand to her lips. If he didn't get through it all, he might not be able to start again. "Except here's the thing. Minor league baseball doesn't pay a lot. The boy barely made a few thousand by the end of the season once he'd paid for food and housing. But he saved every penny he could for his sister."

The light was hitting the dark hair surrounding Anais's face, turning the strands golden in the way that drove him wild.

"Then, finally, after many years, he was so close to his ultimate goal. The big contract, the one that would set him and his sister up for life. The one that would mean they'd never have to use their parents' money or connections again. Then the boy got hurt, and it put everything into jeopardy. In order to get the injury fixed and have a shot at that contract, he'd have to deal with the kind of people he'd avoided for his entire adult life . . . Doctors."

Jackson made a disgusted face and Anais laughed.

"After a few days of boring, stressful appointments with a very fancy doctor in Colorado, he rewarded himself with a nice trip to see his friend in a nearby town. Now, I haven't talked about the girls in this boy's life yet, because there weren't any special ones. He was too focused on that big contract, getting all that money, to have time for girls. But it was more than that. He also—"

Jackson swallowed hard. This was the hard part, the part of himself he was sure she'd push him away for. "He also didn't have anything to offer a girl until he had that contract. His parents had made him believe that he was only worthwhile if he was a doctor."

"Oh, Jackson," Anais breathed, her eyes wide and tender. She put a hand to his face, and he held it there, her touch giving him the courage to keep going with his story.

"He had it in his head that the money and status was what made doctors worthwhile. If he could get that in baseball, then he'd be worthy of love. Not just with a girl, but with his parents too. So when he finally did meet a special girl, he didn't think she'd ever see him as more than something temporary. That she'd never want something more with him until he'd made it big."

"Did the boy figure out this wasn't true?"

"Eventually." He put her hand that was on his face around his neck. "But he did a lot of dumb stuff first."

"Oh yeah?" Anais's lips turned up, and she brought her other hand to join the first, pulling in closer to his face. "Like what?"

"Like agreeing to her ridiculous idea that they hook up in secret when it turned out her brother knew the whole time what was happening."

Anais laughed loudly at this, throwing her head back. "Isabelle had it figured out too."

"It was her cousin that ratted us out to Bastien."

"Oh, I'll get him back for that one . . . " Anais's face turned serious. "What other dumb stuff did the boy do?"

The prickles in his chest took hold, and he pushed them away to say the words he knew were the most important ones.

"He lied to her. He hid the truth about his injury. He was sorry." He shook his head. "I'm sorry, Anais. I just didn't think it was worth it to get into it all when you were leaving for Boston. What did it matter if I might never be able to play again? And that was before Bastien told me it's where you think you'll find love."

"I'm not going to Boston."

"What?" He dropped his arms. "Not because of me, I hope? Because that's even dumber, to change your plans just for some guy—"

"I know." She put a hand to his lips. "I'm sorry I didn't tell you that was the reason why I wanted to go. It was why, I mean, at first, but it was more because it's what my dad had done and it would be best for the town. But it wouldn't be best for me. I was away for years already. I don't want to leave again, even if it's just for a year."

Jackson smiled. "It's good to hear you're thinking of yourself first." His face dropped when he realized what it meant. "I'm still getting the surgery, though. I have to take this shot."

She sighed and leaned her head against his chest.

"I know. And you know I can't follow you wherever you go this year."

"I know." He pressed his lips to her hair, breathed in that lavender scent that he wished he could bottle and take with him. "But I'd still like to try to be together, if you'd want to."

She looked up at him. "Really?"

"Anais, I've never felt about someone the way I've felt these past few weeks with you." He swallowed again, getting ready for more honesty, but this time he was confident she wouldn't react badly to it. "It's probably too early to say it, but I think I lo—"

"I love you too." She reached up and pressed her lips to his, her hands tight on the back of his head.

He laughed as much as he could with his lips smashed against hers, a happy delirious sound that spread warmth throughout his body, helped along by the electricity that was always there between them. It was even better than a grand slam in the last game of a championship. Nothing could top this feeling. His hands tangled in her hair, her tongue warm against his, the smell of her invading his senses. Everything was Anais, and he never wanted to move again.

"I guess I'll come back later for that batting lesson."

They pulled apart, breathless and red-faced, to find Elias staring at them with a giant grin on his face.

"How long have you been standing there?" Anais gave her brother a glare that Jackson hoped would never be pointed in his direction.

"Long enough to know you'll probably be visiting us pretty often. You can show me the trick next time."

With that, Elias ran off, leaving a bemused Jackson and a flustered Anais still wrapped in each other's arms.

He ran a hand down her back. "I don't know what this next year looks like for me."

"That's okay." She smiled up at him. "I'll figure out a plan."

"Of course you will."

Hand in hand, they walked back to the festival.

The Floodline was so packed, Anais could barely see the bar. She spotted Isabelle at a corner table with Tina and squeezed past the crush to get to them.

"Did the freezer break again?"

"No." Isabelle rolled her eyes and Tina snickered. "Matt cut his hand on a glass. Austin patched him up, then decided to stay back there and help serve."

Anais took another look around at the crowd. There were definitely more women than men, she realized. A final look confirmed Clementine wasn't among them, but she did spot her sister Danielle, home for a few days for an interview at Centennial U's medical school.

You can't control everything, she reminded herself with a deep breath before turning back to Isabelle and Tina.

They were halfway through telling her a story about a mixed-up shipment of cookbooks when a deep voice tickled Anais's ears.

"Is this seat taken?"

Barely able to contain her excitement, she jumped up and wrapped her arms around Jackson.

"You were supposed to call so I could pick you up."

His rumbly laugh vibrated through her as he squeezed her hard against his chest. "I like surprising you."

The kiss he gave her was scorching, and only the tiniest part of her worried what people around her were thinking. It was taking time, and regular sessions with a therapist, but the constant anxiety and worry over things she couldn't control were lessening every day.

Which had helped enormously since it had been a year of plans that Anais had changed on an almost daily basis. There'd been Clementine's bombshell announcement about school, followed by an NP deciding not to return after welcoming his third child. Thank goodness Austin had already been on board, helping keep Miller Family Medical running smoothly while Anais dealt with even more uncertainty around Jackson's career.

When Jackson had been put on waivers by the Ospreys not long after getting his surgery and leaving Jasper Creek, there'd been the very real possibility no other team would pick him up. The planning they'd done in those tense forty-seven hours of waiting all revolved around Jackson finishing his degree, so he'd at least have the baseline qualification of a bachelor's. For one glorious night, Anais had let herself picture him going to school in Denver and living in Jasper Creek, the life she'd always wanted starting within weeks rather than years later.

It had been bittersweet for her when he'd called her with the news from Phil about an offer from the major league team in Boston. Giving up the fellowship felt like the worst idea she'd ever had. It was Jackson who'd reminded her that there was no guarantee he'd stay in Boston, and it would be better for her to have her family close when the inevitable happened and he got sent somewhere else.

He'd been right, of course—something she'd only said once

that he'd never let her forget. The next eight months had been a whirlwind of visits back and forth, long weekends, and shouting from the grandstands. It wasn't the life she'd pictured for herself, but she was surprised how much she loved it. Flying out to see Jackson and crashing in his tiny loft apartment in downtown Boston felt just as much like coming home as arriving back in Jasper Creek.

Then, like he'd predicted, Boston had traded him, and he'd ended up in the minors for a team in California. A shoulder injury over the summer made it clear his days as a player were drawing to a close. Whenever his team decided to let him go, he would retire. Anais had pushed hard to make sure it was what he wanted when he'd told her. It was sooner than he'd have preferred, but he had a plan for what came next—even if it changed more often than Anais would have liked.

The plans for this weekend, however, were firm: spend as much time as possible with him before he went to Denver to show his sister around. She had a medical school interview at CU in a week.

"When does Madison get in?" Anais asked, keeping her arm wrapped around him as they sat down at the table.

"Tuesday. Will your sister be gone by then?" He looked over his shoulder at Danielle, dancing with her friends.

"Yeah. It would have been nice for them to meet now, but they can meet at school once they both get in."

"You're in charge of admissions now?" Isabelle raised an eyebrow.

Jackson's lips turned up. "And in charge of what school they decide they go to?"

Anais squirmed. "No, but it's nice to think about, isn't it?"

He planted a quick kiss on her nose. "It's great to think about."

Even if his time in the majors wasn't very long, the boost in pay for the time he'd been on the active roster had been signifi-cant. Not enough to pay for all of Madison's medical degree, but combined with everything he'd been saving over the years, it was enough to make her brave enough to look at a school other than the one her parents had picked out. Only time would tell if she was brave enough to take the leap her brother had.

Matt Hayes, his hand wrapped in gauze, weaved in and out of the crowd to bring their table a round of beer and ice-cream pints.

"I think they'll both pick Denver," Anais said, and took a bite of Moose Tracks.

"They'll pick whatever's right for them, the same way their older siblings did." Jackson put a spoon of Rocky Road in his mouth and let out a satisfied groan.

Anais laughed. "Are you sure you didn't just pick me because of the ice cream in Jasper Creek?"

"Hey, you only picked me because of my favorite movie."

Their teasing continued for the rest of the night, with Isabelle and Tina chiming in, and before long, Danielle and Austin had made their way over to their table.

A year ago, Anais thought the only way she'd ever be happy was to leave the people and places she loved most. The pressure to do what was expected, to follow a set path, had been so over-whelming. Now, she could relax into a version of her life that was messier than she ever thought she'd be able to enjoy.

The ice cream helped quite a bit.

Jackson helped more.

AUTHOR'S NOTE

Whenever I read a romance novel, I always wonder what's real and what's not.

Yes, I realize the entire point of fiction is that it's made up. But there are always hints of real places, people, and events tucked in between the imaginary dialogue uttered by inexplicably buff and beautiful characters.

I made up a lot more than I usually do for this book, in part because it was fun, but also because whenever you use real places/people, you're more limited in what details you can change. Since this is the first in a series that will go on for at least five books, I needed as much control as possible over the details...yes I am a little bit like Anais in that way!

Here's a short and incomplete list of what's real and what's not in this book:

- Jasper Creek, Colorado: not a real town, unfortunately. It sounds like a nice place to live though, doesn't it? The Floodline Brewery in particular sounds like somewhere I'd love to hang out!
- Centennial University Hospital: not a real university or hospital.
- The Weston Wildcats and Olympia Ospreys: not real baseball teams, but the financial struggles of minor league players is very real.

- Hamate fracture: this little bone in your hand is very real, and injuring it is fairly common among athletes.

If you enjoyed *A Shot At Love* then take a peek at *Houseplants & Hardcovers*, a sweet rivals-to-lovers romance with major *You've Got Mail* vibes and tons of plant puns.

Chapter 1

November

JCEdits
Hi! Sorry for the random DM. You've been super helpful in the comments, but my current plant situation has gotten overwhelming.

Plantsguy95
What seems to be the problem? What kind of plants are they?

> **JCEdits**
> Well . . . everything is very, very brown. And they are all, um, green plants? My mother got them for me.

> **Plantsguy95**
> No worries, happy to help with any and all plant problems.

> We'll figure out how to get things back in the green in no time.

APRIL

Pete the prayer plant was dying.

If Juliet was being honest with herself, he had been dying for a while. Then she'd gone into one of her super-concentrated work sprints and did nothing but sleep and copyedit for four days. Now most of her plants looked less than well-loved, sagging sadly over the edge of their pots between teetering stacks of books, but poor Pete had suffered the worst.

Juliet leaned in, examining his leaves in the sunlight streaming through her home office's windows. Unlike Pete, Juliet had gotten some nourishment this week, but only because her mom had sent food over. Almost twenty years since she left home, she still regularly needed to be watered and fed by someone else.

A buzzing from her desk drew her attention away from her plants. Her phone was ringing. She didn't have to look to know it was her mom. No one else called her.

"Did you get the salad?"

"Hello to you too." Juliet tucked the blanket she was wearing over her shoulders even tighter so it draped behind her like a cape. "Yes, I got it."

"Did you eat it?"

"Yes." Not immediately, but within twelve hours. That counted as the same meal, didn't it?

Her mother sighed, as if she'd guessed at Juliet's unspoken words. "It shouldn't be this hard to keep my thirty-seven-year-old daughter alive." The sounds of nature chirped through the phone, along with the babble of a toddler. "Your sister doesn't need this kind of attention. Her small children do."

"So stop sending the salads. I can take care of myself."

"You can't even keep those plants alive."

Juliet had no argument there. Here she was, staring at five shriveled brown leaves on a prayer plant that looked like it was praying to be put out of its misery.

"The plants were your idea. You should be the one to take care of them." The bitterness in her words got another sigh from her mother. Like she needed another reminder about how incompetent she was at managing her own life.

"I water them every time I come over. Or rather, whenever you let me come over."

The itch to get back to her computer and escape this conversation was a thousand writhing ants crawling up her arms. In front of a page, with stylistic errors and typos to be corrected, Juliet was in total control. When online reputations and major financial deals could be ruined forever from a misplaced comma, nothing was more important than the right editor. Her clients' only concern was that she got their manuscripts polished to perfection in record time. They didn't care if she could keep a plant alive.

Juliet tugged gently at the brownest of Pete's leaves, and it slipped off the stem as if attached by only the flimsiest of threads. The prayer plant needed her more than her clients right now, it seemed.

Thank goodness her mother hadn't bought her a cat.

"You can come over tonight, if you want," Juliet said,

turning away from Pete to look at the calendar above her desk. "I just finished a deadline, so I don't have much work for the next few days."

"It'll have to wait, sweetie, Allison needs me to watch the boys overnight."

The sting of rejection shouldn't be as sharp after all these years, but there it was. Her mother complained Juliet never wanted her to come over, but then was too busy when she did invite her. Juliet took a deep breath and the pain in her chest eased a bit, though not completely.

"Well, whenever you have time. I'm always here," she said.

"That's what worries me the most. You should get out of the house more."

"Mom, I work at home."

"Exactly. You live your whole life inside." There was a loud squawk from her mother's end of the phone—one of the kids must have seen a dog or something. "Allison's husband just finished his third Ironman this weekend. He almost qualified for the world championships."

"I know. I saw the pictures." Juliet plopped down in her office chair, curled her legs to her chest, and pulled the blanket over herself.

"You could have seen it in person."

"I had a deadline." Also, it had been a three-hour drive to the mountain town to Tony's race. There was no way she would have been able to do that, even if she still had a car.

"I would have driven you." Again, it was as if her mom had guessed the words she'd held back.

Now if only she could pick up on Juliet's desire to get off the phone and back to her plant disaster.

"Next time. I have to go. I'll call you in a few days."

After saying their goodbyes, Juliet hung up and stood up, the blanket dropping to the floor. Rather than deal with the emotions a five-minute phone call had dredged up, she switched to her camera to take a picture of the dying plant. Then, it was just another swipe of her thumb and a few taps of her fingers to pull open the social media app where normally she'd post about the open space in her editing calendar. Instead, she went into the private-messaging section to send the photo to the one person who could help her right now.

Plantsguy95.

There was already a message waiting for her, a laughing emoji in response to a meme she'd sent him a few days ago. From that initial message a few months ago—when her mother had dropped off five plants and they'd all been drooping within a week—an easy online friendship had blossomed.

Blossomed. She almost groaned out loud at the plant pun. That was undoubtedly his influence. He was funny with words in a way she could never achieve without hours of contemplation first.

The little green dot next to his profile picture—a leafy green *Ficus*—let Juliet know he was online. A reply came almost immediately to her picture of a dying Pete.

Plantsguy95
What happened?

JCEdits
I got busy with work.

Plantsguy95
Isn't this one in the bathroom like I suggested, for the humidity?

Did you not go to the bathroom for a week?

JCEdits
I plead the fifth.

> **Plantsguy95**
> JC, you gotta be nicer to your body. Forget
> about the plants.

Juliet snorted. Though it went against all sorts of best practices for using social media to grow your business, she didn't share her name unless someone was a client. Plantsguy95 only knew her as JCEdits, her username, which he turned into JC.

> **JCEdits**
> I'm screenshotting that and showing all your 15
> million followers you said that.

> **Plantsguy95**
> 15 million?

> Wow, it must have gone up by 14.99 million
> since yesterday.

> **JCEdits**
> You mean you don't check your followers?

> You have like, five times as many as me, and
> people share your stuff all the time.

> **Plantsguy95**
> This isn't my full-time gig.

> It's not even a gig. I don't get paid for this.

> I just want people to learn about plants.

For someone with close to twenty thousand followers, Plantsguy95 had a very laid-back approach to his account that Juliet couldn't understand. Not for the first time, she wondered what his real job was . . . and his name. Neither of them posted pictures of themselves, so she didn't even know what he looked like. All his photos were plants, sometimes with hands she assumed were his, sometimes his shadow. Her account was entirely copyediting tips and memes, her profile photo a stylized red pen.

She knew he was a *he* from the pronouns in his bio, but beyond that, it was frustratingly bare bones, even more anonymous than Juliet's. At least hers told the world what she did and how to contact her. All his said was "I'm a guy who likes plants. I answer your #solvemyplantproblem questions every Wednesday." No location, no link to a website or even a fundraising campaign.

> **JCEdits**
> Thank goodness you aren't trying to get paid for this.
>
> The sloppy copy in your posts would make any legitimate sponsors run for the hills.

> **Plantsguy95**
> Well, you refuse to let me hire you, so I'll just have to struggle along without your expert eyes.

> **JCEdits**
> Can I get your expert eyes on my plant please?
>
> I'll write five posts for free for you if it lives to next week.

> **Plantsguy95**
> Deal.

Juliet never took social media clients, since she charged by word, and it was not the most efficient use of her time. This was a dire situation, however, and exceptions had to be made. Within minutes, he sent a comprehensive list of everything Juliet needed to do, almost hour by hour, to make sure Pete survived. The tension that had built up over the last four days dropped off Juliet's shoulders. It was reassuring to see something so organized. Now that she felt like the plant part of her life was under control, she could get back to work.

Lucas was in the middle of his shift at the hardware store when he got an update from JC about the prayer plant she'd ignored into drought. It was still drooping a week after he'd told her how to save it, but "since it's technically still alive," she said he could send her the posts he wanted her to write.

His lips curved up into a smile wider than the hacksaws he was pricing as he tapped out a reply.

Plantsguy95
Are you sure your prayer plant doesn't have a death wish?

JCEdits
The thought has crossed my mind. I thought I was a good roommate.

No complaints from the others, though.

Plantsguy95
How many others do you have?

JCEdits
Roommates or plants?

Plantsguy95
I already know how many plants you have, since I've had to keep them all from dying from lack of attention.

JCEdits
And how many is that?

Plantsguy95
10.

JCEdits
Ha! I have 12 plants.

I kept the Aloe plants alive all by myself.

Plantsguy95
I'm positively bursting with pride.

JCEdits
Don't get too proud, you haven't saved the prayer plant yet.

She'd avoided the roommate question, and while it might not have been intentional, it did remind him that she wasn't that kind of online friend. Personal details shared were minimal. They never talked much about family or friends. She only mentioned her work when it got in the way of her plant care.

Leaning against a shelf full of boxes of nails, Lucas ran a hand through his hair and stared down at his phone, like he could hypnotize it into giving him the information he wanted.

The internet was an amazing thing. You could look up the answers to literally any question, as Lucas liked to remind his family when they blew up his phone with their bonkers requests at three in the morning. Though at least his grandmother waited until the sun was up.

The internet, however, could not solve the question he'd been wondering about for months, despite the embarrassing amount of hours he'd spent sleuthing.

Who was JCEdits?

All he knew for sure was that she was an editor. A few years ago, he would have traded all his plant advice until the end of time to get professionally written and edited posts. What had started as a failed side hustle had turned into an unexpected way to connect with other plant nerds outside of his small town. It wasn't to make money or get famous, at least not anymore. Not since his ex—and his reason for starting the account—was no longer in the picture. Now, he just wanted to talk to people about plants and help them learn more about them.

A few short months ago, JC had been completely clueless. Even worse than his cousin Marigold—Mari—who'd managed to kill a cactus in two days by mixing up the saltwater she'd put in a bottle for her facial routine with . . . well, it didn't really matter since he'd told her at least five times succulents don't need daily watering.

JC was a quick learner though. Since Lucas loved nothing more than people who asked him questions about the things he loved most, they'd been chatting a few times a week since her first timid message asking for help with her brand-new plant babies.

It was nice, in a way, to have something that was light and low pressure. The opposite of his life with a huge family that lived and breathed drama like they were trying out to be the next reality TV sensation.

And yet . . . he really wanted to know if JC lived with anyone.

Instead of asking again, he looked up from his phone to make sure he was still alone in the aisle, and focused his response to her on the plants, like he was expected to.

Plantsguy95
Why don't you try your local horticultural society?

JCEdits
I'm sorry, my local what now?

This isn't the 1800s and I am not a romance
heroine with nothing to do until an appropriate
suitor comes to call.

Plantsguy95
Fine, garden club, if you prefer.

JCEdits
Also not a 1950s housewife waiting for her
husband to come home to beat him over the
head with a leg of lamb.

He chuckled, and the noise caught his boss's attention.
Normally, Henry didn't care about phone use during work. But
whenever Henry's dad, who owned the store, was around, the
rules suddenly became stricter. So Lucas stashed his phone in
his back pocket and got back to pricing boxes of nails under
Henry's watchful eye. It was an agonizing three hours before
Lucas could reply to JC's message.

His shift finally over, Lucas practically threw his apron at
Henry and ran out of the hardware store, passing a row of
smaller shops on his way to the back parking lot that employees
used. The evening was warm for early spring, and he inhaled a
lungful of crisp air as he leaned against the side of his truck and
thought about what to tell JC. It was a fine line to walk between
revealing too much about himself and coming off as insincere.

The choice to never show his face in the account kept him
anonymous. Plants were his main focus on the account, not
making it his identity, his business, his life. That hadn't gone
very well the first time he'd tried it, as the harsh criticisms of his
ex had so generously pointed out.

Besides, Greenhaven was on the smaller side. Five square
miles with an adorable store-lined, cobblestone main street that

would make Norman Rockwell proud, and a gossip mill that put Hollywood tabloids to shame. Lucas knew word would get around if he put his face out there, then *everyone* would have something to say about it. It was enough trouble as it was to have his younger cousins weigh in on his very outdated use of hashtags.

Now, however, he wished he could tell JC about the garden club in Greenhaven that he'd belonged to since he was old enough to hold a spade.

Plantsguy95
Google the name of your city + horticultural society or garden club, to see what comes up.

Most cities of a certain size have one, even if it's just a few people who get together to trade seeds.

JCEdits
"Trade seeds" huh?

Is that what the kids these days are calling it?

He laughed out loud at that one, then looked around to make sure no one had seen him. Laughing to himself in a deserted parking lot behind Main Street wasn't exactly his best look. Not to mention if Henry spotted him, he'd probably assume Lucas had nowhere to be tonight and ask him to work a few more hours.

Before he could forget, he drafted a post on garden clubs to share with his followers, giving a bit of the history and importance that they served in communities. It took an enormous amount of restraint to not add anything specific to his town, since he honestly thought they were one of the best in his area. The work they did in Greenhaven was incredible, and not just because his family had done so much of it.

Now dangerously close to having Henry come out and ask him to help close the store, Lucas got into his truck—even years after he passed, it was still hard to not think of it as his grandfather's old truck—to drive to his grandmother's house. On his way, he passed town hall, where the rows of planters were fresh and colorful thanks to the club. Two people chatted away on the nearby bench as the sky turned darker, oblivious to the months of fundraising the garden club had done to get it installed.

Typical. He sighed as he turned onto a side street. *No one appreciates a really good garden.*

There was a family crossing the street to the library, which was lit up inside for some evening event, and Lucas stopped the truck to let them pass. A few buildings down, his cousin Sage's car was parked in front of the garden club, and a light was on.

Their grandmother was still the elected president of the Greenhaven Garden Club, but she'd gotten sick over the winter. Then her best friend had died, and Granny just didn't seem to like being out and about as much. They'd scheduled an election for the next meeting to select an acting president, but for now, the other members rotated duties.

Except Sage wasn't technically a member. She was family, and the Geis family helped each other no matter what. So without a second's hesitation, Lucas pulled into the driveway behind her car, whatever plans he'd had for the evening put on hold in favor of something much more important.

HOUSEPLANTS
AND HARDCOVERS
A SWEET RIVALS TO LOVERS ROMANCE
DAPHNE JAMES HUFF

ABOUT THE AUTHOR

Daphne James Huff has been writing romance for adult and YA audiences since she was a young adult herself. Her favorite kind of story has a main character who thinks they've got it all figured out until someone barges into their life and messes everything up (Translation: Give her all the enemies-to-lovers books, please!).

Daphne works in HR during the day and fills her nights with reading, baking, and practicing whichever sport she's fallen in love with most recently (2022 was her year of inline skating).

When she's not writing, she enjoys partaking in her hobbies with her husband, son, and cat (though finding skates that will fit the cat has been a bit difficult).

(There are not this many parentheses in her books . . . usually.)

Follow her on Instagram **@daphnejameshuff**